UNHOLY TEMPTATION

SINFUL NATURES 4

LYNN BURKE

1

———

JED

"How's my baby boy?"

The comfort of Mom's voice eased some of the tension riding my shoulders. "Exhausted," I muttered, climbing out of my car.

"Renee called and told me Mrs. Jenkins passed away."

The secretary I shared with Pastor Welker enjoyed chatting about the church's going-ons, and with her being Mom's best friend, I wasn't surprised by the call. Mom always checked in with me whenever the gossip mill churned up drama.

"Yeah, this morning," I managed past the tightness in my throat.

The devastation of Mr. Jenkins and their three young children had hit me hard while I'd visited with them that afternoon. Blank stares, some tears, and one angry twelve-year-old screaming curses at God for taking their mommy from them.

"Your Dad and I are praying for you, Jed."

I swiped my suit coat over my stinging eyes. "Thanks, Mom."

"Call me later if you need to chat, okay?"

We said our goodbyes, and I let out a heavy exhale, ready to shed my suit and the heaviness in my heart.

While having a high level of empathy was a great thing for an assistant pastor, some days I struggled beneath the weight of the life I'd chosen.

At least the sun hung longer in the sky, chasing the gloom of winter behind.

I paused in my walk to my apartment building, lifting my face for a kiss of warmth—the only caress of affection outside my family that brought happiness to my soul. Soaking in a few seconds of rays and three deep cleansing breaths eased some of the grief I'd dealt with that day.

The slam of a heavy door pulled my eyes open.

A moving truck sat near the front entrance a couple hundred yards away, two men conversing at the pull-down door by its rear.

The taller of the two stood with his back to me, his wide shoulders and dark hair reminding me of my first and only crush. He'd been gone sixteen years but still haunted my mind.

I turned toward the side entryway, not having the emotional strength to linger on the past and the last night I'd seen Aiden McNelis, my brother's best friend.

Their college graduation party had been the one time I'd hugged someone besides a family member, and I could still feel the strength of his arms that had felt so right.

Like I'd been born to be his.

Eighteen, and I'd known in the deepest parts of my soul that I would love Aiden and him alone until I breathed my last.

Pushing aside my fondest and saddest memory, I let myself into the building's side entrance and began the trek up three flights of stairs. With every step, I imagined shedding the cares of the day until all that remained was a worn-out single male who needed some dinner and his favorite fuzzy socks.

I shuffled down the hallway, digging my keys from my slacks' pocket while clutching my briefcase in the other hand.

Footfalls sounded far behind me, but I didn't have the emotional energy to turn and make small talk with whichever neighbor approached.

The hairs on my nape stood on end as a tingle crept down my spine.

"Padawan?"

My heart stuttered and raced at the nickname

only one person had ever called me. His voice suggested cigarette use even though he'd refused to touch cancer sticks. The perfect aphrodisiac to my ears.

Surely they deceived me.

I stared at my apartment door. The exhaustion of the day weighed my shoulders down, probably prompting my mind to play tricks on me.

"Padawan?"

The same voice—*Aiden*.

Adrenaline coursed through me, waking my senses and sending shivers over my skin as the raspy tone had done since I was a kid.

Swallowing hard, I turned, taking in the six-foot-plus gorgeous man striding toward me.

The man from the truck, I realized.

A tight T-shirt stretched over his broad shoulders, but more girth swelled his prominent pecs than when he'd been twenty-two. Gym shorts cradled a bulge I tore my eyes from for a quick glance of muscular thighs and calves.

Aiden was and always had been an unholy temptation in physical form, a god-like being blessing the rest of humanity with his presence.

His smirks while winking at me and his laughter had brought my body to life like nothing else.

My one and only...

"Shit. It *is* you." He grinned while I stared, struck dumb.

He had become my obsession from the first time I'd seen his twinkling hazel eyes and tousled dark hair. So beautiful my belly had flipped and my knees swooned whenever we'd been in close proximity.

Aiden had appeared in my first wet dream at age fourteen and continued to haunt me when I chose not to masturbate for months on end.

Heat flooded through me, settling in my groin and face as he closed the distance between us. Pulse pounding between my ears, I licked some moisture to my suddenly dry lips, my hands clenching my bag and keys with a death grip at my sides.

"Aiden..." I coughed to cover how I'd croaked his name. "Wh-what are you doing here?"

I sounded like a squeaky kid.

He stepped right into my personal space and yanked me up into his arms, taking my feet clear off the ground. Easy to do since he towered over me by a good eight inches.

My heart threatened to burst, but I soaked in the feel of his hard chest, every swell and dip, crushing against my much smaller one. Delicious, subtle cologne, more citrus than spice, replaced the Axe he used to bathe in as a teen. Strong biceps squeezed me while I selfishly took the moment to breathe him in and glory in his touch.

Countless times, the memory of our first hug had flashed inside my head, my body stirring with desire until I gave myself release, then felt guilty for my sinful lust.

Same as that night, he tempted my groin to react, but Aiden set me back on my feet before I swelled fully and embarrassed the heck out of myself.

"It's good to see you, kid."

Kid.

But his grin, those eyes full of laughter, made me not care so much that he saw me that way.

I slid my briefcase in front of me to keep from embarrassment, stood as tall as possible on shaking legs, and lifted my chin. I was nothing more than a shadow beside the virility he emanated. With my build, slim no matter the muscle I gained, I would have been considered a twink while in my twenties.

At thirty-four, I still couldn't grow a beard to save my life and only had to shave once every three days or so.

"It's good to see you too, Aiden. What are you doing here?" I repeated, sounding somewhat normal even though my insides hurled around like a tsunami.

A brief furrow lined his brow, the happiness from earlier fading a bit. "Jacob didn't tell you I was moving home?"

It would have been nice to be prepared, but leave it to my brother to forget to fill me in.

"He hasn't mentioned it, no. Wife. Kids. The job."

I offered excuses for Jacob, shrugging as though unbothered by how we'd grown apart.

"Shannon and I split up," Aiden said, his tone bland, his eyes emptier than I'd ever remembered seeing.

Loneliness, I realized—and recognized inside myself.

"I'm sorry to hear that." I meant the words since Aiden would never be anything but a secret fantasy of mine, and I had wanted him to find happiness with whoever he loved.

"Don't be," Aiden said, gesturing his hand as though he'd left her in his past with no qualms, but a shadow lingered on his face as he glanced away. "I decided to come back to the only place that felt like home to start over again."

He's here to stay.

I smiled, my insides settling somewhat from the initial shock of seeing him in the flesh. "Welcome back, then."

Aiden dug a key from his pocket and held it up. "Looks like we're neighbors." He tipped his head to the door directly across from my apartment.

My breath left in another rush as I imagined how often we would run into each other—and what it would do to my libido on a daily basis.

"Get outta town," I muttered, that heat flushing through me again.

"Just got here, kid. I'd rather stick around for a

while." His smirk and familiar teasing wink brought to life the butterflies I hadn't felt in ages.

"What are the chances?" I asked with a huff while shaking my head, wanting to faint and curse at the same time.

Aiden shrugged, his gaze flitting over my button-down shirt and slacks. "Fate ordained it."

"Or perhaps God did," I suggested and immediately bit my tongue. It was more likely the devil's work since my new neighbor would be nothing but an enticement to the sinful nature I'd easily ignored for countless years.

Why, God? How could you allow this to happen to me?

After Aiden had left for California, I'd followed in the footsteps of Gramps and Grandpa, hoping He would change my sexual longings to that of a normal person.

But that prayer had gone unanswered too.

Even if desiring a man aligned with what I'd been taught since a child, Aiden had been like a third son to my parents, and any relationship outside platonic would have been seen as incestuous if found out.

Family was everything to me, my niece and nephew the little loves of my life since I knew I would never have children of my own. Their mother Trish was like the sister I'd always wanted with her tender kindness and affectionate nature.

Stepping outside the world I'd been raised in would rip all I'd known to shreds, and I couldn't have that.

"Jacob told me you became a pastor." Aiden studied my face as though looking for something, but I had no clue what that might be.

I'd always been the pious one of the Simpson boys, the quiet and nurturing to Jacob's wild and uninhibited spirit. It only seemed right I would follow in both our grandfather's footprints in becoming ordained.

Mom and Dad telling me all the time how they took pride in their son who chose the ministry gave me a sense of having done right—even if I didn't feel true to myself.

"Assistant pastor," I said, "at Simply Grace Church."

The study of my face continued long enough I shifted in my dress shoes, more than ready to get out of my work clothes and pull on some sweats.

Who was I kidding?

I wanted to escape the citrus scent in my nose, the flutters in my belly...the need to hold my bag in front of me to hide what Aiden's closeness did to my libido.

If not for Aiden, I would have labeled myself asexual. No one else had ever lit desire to life inside me, only memories of his younger face and the way he'd strutted around shirtless whenever Mom and Dad weren't home.

Palpitations fluttered my heart over memories of his chest I'd never got to touch. Kiss. Bite.

"When did you move in?" I managed to get words out without revealing my arousal.

"Just finished and sent the moving truck on its way."

"Do you have dinner plans?" I spewed without thought and immediately cursed in my head over the possible consequences to my poor body.

His slow smirk sent another rush of butterflies through my core.

Definitely a mistake.

"Is that an invite?"

"Pizza," I blurted when I should have taken back what I'd tossed out. "With ham and—"

"Pineapple," we both said at the same time.

Smiles rose on both our faces, easing some of the tension in my shoulders.

But none from my aching groin.

"Sounds good to me, Jed."

Not kid, not Padawan.

My heart sang, and my pulse thrummed as my lips stretched into a full-on grin. Mistake or not, I wasn't about to retract my offer of dinner and catch up with Aiden. I would enjoy the sight of him, hide away memories to dream about—and eventually repent after I allowed those fantasies to dictate the actions of my sinful nature.

"An hour?" I suggested.

"It's a date." Aiden winked and turned to unlock his door.

My gaze dropped to his backside and the shorts hanging off his narrow hips. His ass hadn't changed.

The round globes made me want to bite a juicy apple.

My mouth watering, I spun on my heel, jamming my key into the lock—and imagining a different type of insertion.

Damnit.

Swallowing hard, I hurried into my apartment, shut the door, and leaned against it. My bag hit the floor, my head tipped back, and my eyes closed.

Why?

The only word I could whisper before God's throne, but same as every time I prayed, I didn't hear a peep of an answer.

Living by faith was incredibly hard. Prayer didn't give direction. The Bible didn't work like Siri did with his sexy British accent whenever I asked *him* a question.

I filled my lungs to capacity and slowly let my exhale leak between my parted lips, telling myself I had to calm my libido back down to its usual status of six feet under.

But I could still smell Aiden.

It was like his cologne stuck in my nose hairs, lingering. Enticing. And the sight of his face behind my closed eyelids...I'd thought he was hot in his early twenties. Thirty-eight looked damn fine on the man, the slight lines bracketing his mouth and the corners of his eyes making him even more appealing to me.

Obsession in human form, one I wouldn't be able to avoid.

I didn't *want* to.

"I'm in trouble," I muttered to myself.

My groin throbbed, and I glanced over the tent in my slacks. I didn't pack a lot down there, but considering I rarely saw the sight I observed, it appeared obnoxious in its lust for a man.

But not exactly unwanted and in my opinion, far from disgusting as I'd been taught from childhood.

I slid my trembling hand over myself and let out a whimper. It had been too long since I experienced an erection—even longer since I bowed down to need and gave myself release.

Aiden is coming over for pizza. Here. In my apartment—just the two of us.

That thought sent me scurrying toward the bathroom, and I tore off my suit as I went, leaving pieces on the floor in my wake. Coat and tie landed in the kitchen within two steps. Shirt and belt in my bedroom doorway. Slacks, briefs, and the thin socks

I hated ended up in a line leading toward the room I would hide in while jerking off.

Nothing would ease the ache except ejaculating, and I couldn't wait for the shower's cold spray to warm up. I hopped right in, squirted conditioner on my palm, and took myself in hand, my breath in gasps as though I'd been out jogging for an hour.

"Damn." I clenched my teeth, determined to keep the other curses in my mind from escaping my mouth.

My balls seized up tight against my groin, uncaring of the chilly water raining down over my shoulders. Hand pumping, hips jerking...five seconds later, I erupted without having to imagine anything but Aiden's eyes peering down at me as though trying to read into my soul.

A guttural cry ripped from me at the first shot of cum that splattered on the shower wall. Countless others joined, every throb in my groin weakening my legs until I sagged forward, sucking oxygen into my starved lungs.

Still, I came in dribbled spurts until I trembled and went limp.

Knees giving in, I sank to the shower floor, thankful the water warmed on my head and face. A pleasant buzz lazed through the blood still thumping in my ears, and I closed my eyes, soaking in the sense of euphoria, the tingles racing over my skin and settling into my fingertips and toes.

An addictive feeling I'd thanked God for taking away from me for so long, but with Aiden's return, same as when I'd been younger, I knew I wouldn't be able to set aside my desire for him.

Letting out a heavy exhale, I ran my hands over my hair, tipping my head back. Hot water pinged off my face, my eyelids, and my nose, and I held still until I needed breath again.

I got my feet beneath me and scrubbed before using my luffa to wipe down the mess I'd made on the wall. All evidence of my sinful spend swirled down the drain, and I climbed out and dried off on wobbly legs.

I hadn't come that hard in...years, and even though the sense of sweet release remained, guilt pricked at the back of my mind. I avoided my reflection in the mirror, thinking it might help ease my conscience.

It didn't.

Sexual perversion.

Two words I'd heard countless times from Pastor Welker and the pulpit I'd submitted to echoed in my head.

I offered up a quick prayer of repentance, not even knowing if God listened.

"You're a man now, Jedediah Simpson, not some horny teenager," I muttered to myself while pulling on new boxers and a pair of sweats. "You can exercise restraint and be his friend."

Eat pizza, play catch up, maybe watch a Star Wars movie like we used to do back when we were kids.

It would have to be enough because I'd chosen to dedicate my life to God no matter how much my body would have preferred worshiping Aiden.

Grab your copy of today!

2

AIDEN

I watched over my shoulder as Jed scurried into his apartment and shut the door without a backward glance. The scent of his shampoo was still in my nose, reminding me of sunscreen and the beach.

Coconuts.

Strangely, my mouth watered at the thought of the sweet fruit.

The kid always had a thing for me, and even though no one else seemed to notice, I had. Accidentally on purpose, I'd often gone shirtless if Jacob's mom and dad weren't around, my chest swelling at how Jed checked me out with covert side-eye glances.

Jed had tried to hide his crush all those years ago until Jacob's and my graduation night when he'd hugged me. Looking back, I realized he fit a little too well in my arms—and I'd liked the feeling of him being there.

And when he had lifted his face that night and met my gaze head-on for the first time *ever*? He'd peered up at me as though I hung the stars and moon in the sky—and my insides unsettled in a way I hadn't understood.

Jed was Jacob's little brother, almost like one to me too, so I'd figured the unease inside me that night had been due to that fact. Leaving without seeing him again had made the strange reaction a shit ton easier to deal with, and I'd moved on.

Forgetting.

Finding a new life, other people, to occupy my mind.

Shannon.

My jaw clenched at the thought of my ex-wife, and I turned to let myself into my new apartment. I'd returned east after a nasty divorce from a spiteful woman I'd fallen desperately in love with. My heart still ached even though I put on a front, weariness with the whole affair and with myself for selling my business in a private sale hanging over my shoulders.

I hadn't been lying when I'd said I returned to the only place that felt like home, but it wasn't Philadelphia that had pulled at my heart. It'd been the memory of the friends and family I'd left behind to chase my dreams of doing graphic design in Hollywood where everyone's dreams supposedly came true.

It wasn't for *my* family, either. Sure, my parents were great and all to me and my two sisters, but they had their own life, caught up in their retirement community farther south from where we'd lived when I was younger.

Jacob wasn't the same kid I'd left sixteen years earlier either. He'd settled down, had the wife and kids I'd always wanted, and had remained a faithful attendee of the church where Jed had chosen to work at.

A good-looking guy who was still pint-sized and...a pastor.

Single.

And I would have sworn since I'd met him, gay.

I shook my head, still not understanding his choice of profession, but I knew he'd been pushed to go into the ministry by his grandfathers and parents, the same as Jacob had been.

I'd assumed him to be into guys, me especially, after that hug and silent declaration of his feelings in his dark eyes all those years ago. I'd fled the scene, the state, but wondered how I would deal with it since fate had all but dropped us on each other's laps once more.

Imagining Jed sitting on me, straddling my thighs, sent a ping of adrenaline through my bloodstream and a tingle of something strange down my spine. I frowned while tossing my keys onto my kitchen counter. I wasn't gay, never had found a man even slightly attractive, so it couldn't be that.

But why did my head—both of them—go there? My dick had twitched when I'd gotten carried away from seeing Jed and yanked him clear up off the floor. He'd felt like home against my chest, same as all those years ago.

Not unease...

Interest?

Shaking my head, I focused on what was in front of me to take my mind off whatever Jed stirred inside me. Two boxes of kitchen items and a few bags of stable groceries I'd picked up sat on the countertop.

Furniture lay scattered around the apartment, and my bed from the guest room Shannon and I had in our house piled in pieces. Same as my marriage had been reduced to thanks to her.

My jaw ached as I strode toward the bedroom, needing to at least get that bit of moving-in taken care of so I had a place to crash after hanging with Jed who'd appeared knocked off-kilter by my appearance.

I wondered why Jacob hadn't told him I was coming back east. Jacob and I had drifted apart a bit, but he represented a piece of my life I'd always thought of as a solid foundation. We'd been attached at the hip as kids, which was the only reason I'd gone to youth group with him when he'd asked me to, but how would we fit into one another's lives considering the men we'd become since those days?

While connecting my bed frame, I weighed the main change between us.

Me.

I'd left the church behind, all things God that Jacob's family had introduced me to as a teenager, and had become a flaming liberal. Jacob's Christianity had always been the base of his life even when we had partied it up back in college.

Would we even get along anymore? We'd only spoken on the phone a few times in the past couple of years, that last of which when I'd told him I was moving back to his neck of the woods.

But I hadn't shared the reasons behind my return other than a nasty divorce I'd claimed to put behind me as easily as I'd done his God.

I wished.

Still frowning, I made my bed with the new sheets and comforter I'd picked up the night before. Staying at the house with my ex-wife until the day I'd taken off hadn't been an easy choice, but I'd been unsure of where I headed. Aimless for days on end once our divorce finalized—it'd been Shannon who suggested I go back to where I'd come from before I'd ruined her life.

The bitch didn't say goodbye before I drove off. She hadn't even been around the house I'd allowed her to have without stipulation.

Hot water pounded on me a few minutes later, and I groaned, sagging beneath the weight of bullshit she'd tossed at me over the previous couple of years. Unfulfilling. Workaholic. Lousy lay.

If only the memories of our wasted time together could swirl down the drain like dirtied water.

Releasing a heavy exhale, I stretched my neck side to side, once more telling myself I was moving on. How many men could claim a fresh start at thirty-eight? Thanks to the local gym and needing an escape from our house, I was in the best shape of my life. I also wasn't hurting too badly for money even though the bitch had attempted to wring me dry.

As for my libido? The truck driver and I had hit bars every night while traveling across the US, and while he'd gotten lucky a couple of times, no one interested me enough I could be selfish enough to just get myself off.

God knew—and Shannon let me know—I sucked at pleasing a woman in bed.

Maybe my libido would return with the right person. Maybe someone would give me the chance to learn their body. Maybe they would enjoy what Shannon hadn't—my kisses and the affection I craved to lavish on another.

A catch, Mom called me, but even the thought of trying to date again, hooking up with a stranger in an attempt to disprove Shannon's accusations and reestablish my self-esteem exhausted me. I hoped once the stress from the previous six months, the divorce, the move across the country settled, my desire to connect with someone, even if just for a physical release, would return.

I pulled on a clean pair of shorts and T-shirt, actually excited to head over to Jed's for pizza. It would be my first step at home to re-right my life and find some peace and quiet in my head and heart.

Since Jacob wasn't available and I had dinner plans with my parents later in the week, Jed was naturally the next best choice.

Fate, for once, had been good to me, allowing such a neighbor.

Sweet and kind, Jed would never put me down.

Funny how my heart beat quicker at the thought of spending time alone with him. That slight unease returned, but not enough to make me pass on his invite.

Besides, a man couldn't go wrong with pineapple on pizza.

Shannon had hated the Hawaiian combo, and I hadn't indulged in years. I aimed for my door and pulled up short in the kitchen. As a pastor, I doubted Jed would have cold beer in his fridge, and if I was going to have a total cheat meal...

"Can't have one without the other," I muttered

and grabbed the two cans of beer I had left before heading across the hall.

Jed wouldn't meet my gaze as he opened his door but kept his focus on my chest.

Same as he'd always done.

Shy little guy.

His cheeks flushed like when he'd first noticed me an hour earlier.

I grinned over the thought I should have gone without a shirt and handed him a can while moving past him into his apartment. "Want one?"

"Um...no?" He shut the door behind me, his answer not very precise.

"You sure?" I asked, putting the beer beneath his nose when he turned.

Jed rubbed his palms down his sweats. "No thanks."

"Your loss," I stated with a shrug.

"I wouldn't know." He flicked his focus up at my face and away again just as fast.

"Are you shitting me?" A snort of disbelief escaped me, but I shouldn't have been surprised. The kid had been nothing but straitlaced even as a teenager.

Jed shook his head and weaseled around me without brushing against my body for the kitchen. A coconut-scented cloud wafted past my nose, causing my mouth to water.

I followed on his heels, a quick glance letting me

know he'd grown up somewhat since I'd seen him last even though he wore fluffy socks like back then —but plain blue rather than cartoon-covered. While still on the slight side, Jed had put on some muscle weight. His small but firm ass flexed with every step—

The fuck?

I ripped my focus off Jed's backside and glanced around his apartment instead, looking for something to take my mind off that twinge in my groin again, what I had no business thinking about.

Set up like mine, Jed's kitchen and living area spread open as a single area, but he had one bedroom compared to my two.

"I guess I don't have to offer you something to drink." Jed pulled his fridge open and bent over to grab a bottle of water.

My throat went dry, and I deepened my frown as I once more had to remove my attention from his tight little ass. "Nope, I'm good."

"You can put the other beer in here if you want." Jed stood and held out his hand.

Our fingers brushed as I gave him the second beer, and he must have felt the same tingles race up his arm as I had because his breath caught.

That zap went straight to my dick, stirring me to life.

What the fuck is going on down there?

Face red, Jed spun to put my second beer in the

fridge then scurried to pull out some paper plates and napkins while I tried to work out my body's reaction to him. "Pizza should be here any sec—"

A knock sounded, and Jed scampered around me.

He moved like a damn jackrabbit with a fox on its tail while I stared after him, my brain on shutdown mode.

While he paid the delivery guy, I sifted through the weird vibes I had going nuts in my mind and body.

Exhaustion, I reasoned it away. *Lack of intimacy for too damn long, the comfort of being with someone I've always considered family.*

But Jed wasn't that any longer. We hadn't stayed in touch once I'd left Philly, and I didn't know anything about the man he'd become.

He turned, our gazes once more catching, jacking up my heart rate

No denying he'd become a good-looking man. I imagined him walking into a gay bar and getting hit on by every single guy there.

My frown returned.

Clearing my throat, I sat at his table while he served us a couple of slices each. Steam still rose from the pie, and I leaned forward, filling my lungs rather than focusing on what I was sure had been a twinge of jealousy.

"Damn, that smells good," I all but groaned the

words, my hands getting grabby.

Jed joined me while I shoved the damn pizza in my face—he bowed his head.

I tried not to moan and smack my lips over the sweetness and saltiness exploding across my tongue while he silently prayed.

Over pizza.

Again, I shouldn't have been surprised, but I studied his dark lashes and slashed eyebrows... almost black hair trimmed neatly around his ears and shorter on the sides, a few longer pieces falling over his brow.

I curled my fingers around my pizza rather than reaching across the table to sweep the strands back.

A slight shadow lay along his jawline, the only hint of scruff on his cheeks. I doubted he used a razor more than twice a week, the lucky fucker. I'd eventually given up the struggle to keep clean-shaven, allowing myself a close-trimmed scruff Shannon hadn't ever liked the looks of.

Bitterness ate at my guts like acid, but Jed opened his eyes and caught me staring. The hint of interest sent strange vibes through my body, fading my ex to the back of my mind.

One blink, and he turned his attention on his dinner, swallowing hard while picking up his pizza. "You'd think as a pastor who visits people three out of five days a week for work, I'd know what to say to you."

He took a small bite, the way his lips moved while chewing holding my focus.

"I'm an old friend. Shouldn't be that hard." I bit back a smirk as he all but choked and squirmed in his seat.

I wondered how *hard*—

"I've never had a man—anyone—in my apartment before."

My attention jerked up to his eyes as he refused to look at me.

A few seconds passed as I processed his words. He ate his pizza while mine lay in my hands, forgotten. "No one? Ever?"

Jed swallowed and used a paper napkin to wipe grease from the corner of his mouth. "Outside my parents and Jacob's family once, no."

"No women?" I couldn't help but ask.

"No," he answered quickly, that flush on his cheeks again.

I liked the color. Perhaps a bit too much.

Shifting on my chair, I decided to not push him to out his sexuality—which held no bearing on my life.

"Tell me what you've been up to the last sixteen years, Jed," I said and finally focused on my pizza, determined to get over this...*thing*...that was causing my insides to twitch.

"I went to Bible college, got a job, and moved in here. I go to church services twice a week and visit with my parents every Sunday for our family dinner."

Abrupt and to the point, Jed revealed his private ways hadn't changed since his teenage years.

The poor guy.

"Sandy still insists on those family meals, huh?" I asked about his mom.

Jed nodded while chewing. He wouldn't look at me.

I'd always thought he was just a nervous, shy kid, but having expanded my world, having lived a wild lifestyle when I'd first gotten to California, I knew better.

I made Jed Simpson nervous because his crush hadn't waned in sixteen years.

My body fed off how his attention made me feel. Desired—and better than I had in too fucking long.

I just wasn't sure what to do with the truth that I kind of liked the strange vibes stirring inside me and my groin.

3
____

JED

For the first time in...I couldn't remember how long, no loneliness hovered over my head while eating my dinner. But I wasn't sure the antsy feeling of being in Aiden's presence was more enjoyable.

Even recently sated, my groin considered him being a guest a reason to refuse rest. Aiden made me hard just by being nearby, and there was nothing I could do about it.

Thankful for the table hiding another obnoxious erection, I fought to pay attention to our discussion, but it seemed every other thing he said could be taken as a sexual inuendo even if he hadn't meant to be suggestive.

My heart raced, and I couldn't find calm in the storm he created inside me.

"Tell me about you, Aiden," I said, still unable to face him. I would out myself for sure if he got a good look into my eyes.

"Jacob hasn't kept you updated on my life?"

"My brother is too caught up in his own to think about what might interest me." Heat rushed over me as I realized the opening I'd given him for yet another bit of teasing.

"I interest you?" He smirked, I didn't doubt—I could hear it in his voice, damn him.

"You were part of our family for four solid years." I tried a throwaway reason that wouldn't be laughable. "Of course, I've wondered about you."

"Awe...Padawan missed me."

"I'm not a child, Aiden." I shot him a glare without thought, and those damn orbs of his twinkled, tempting me to lose my head over him.

"Still a Star Wars fanatic?" he asked and turned his attention back to his pizza, but not a hint of *sorry* lined his face.

Thank goodness I kept all my childhood treasures in my bedroom. Behind the closed door. To anyone entering my apartment, I would appear to be a boring bachelor rather than a weirdo.

I tipped my chin up even though he didn't look at me. "Yes."

"Have you seen the Han Solo movie?"

I nodded while finishing my slice of pizza I didn't have much appetite for. "Mmm-hmm."

"Any good?"

"It's my favorite, actually."

Aiden cracked open his can of beer and chugged some down.

My gaze snagged on his Adam's apple as it moved...bobbing beneath scruff and skin.

The ache in my balls pulled my focus off him, and I got another slice of pizza from the box for something to do rather than out of hunger. "More?" I asked as his can clinked onto the table.

"Oh yeah."

"So...*Solo*," I said, sliding another piece of pizza onto his plate. "I have it on Blu-Ray, but I'm sure you want to get unpacked and settled in."

"Dinner dates are always better if there's a movie involved. Unpacking can wait."

Date.

There he went with that word again, but I wouldn't know what being on one felt like. I certainly wasn't about to tell him that fact over his continued joke though. It had been bad enough I'd shocked him by admitting to not having anyone but family step over my threshold in all the years I'd lived in the apartment.

"Do you still draw?" I asked, going to a safer, less intrusive conversation.

"Doodle," he corrected, "and not really. Most of my creativity is done on a computer these days."

"That's a shame. I've yet to meet someone who does cartoon characters like you."

I'd stolen one of his sketchbooks the night before he'd left for California—and it lay in my bedstand drawer beneath...well, a few other things I hadn't thought about for months.

"What about your writing?" Aiden asked while I fought the need to fidget, praying the red away from my face. "Still secretly dreaming about publishing a sci-fi book someday?"

"I set that aside when I went to Bible college."

Aiden sat silent, and I felt his stare long enough I squirmed in my seat. "Has it been worth it, Jed? Giving up your passion, your dreams, to live by faith in a being who doesn't speak or show his face?"

His blunt question hit my chest with enough force to steal the air from my lungs.

Because I'd asked myself that dozens of times over the years.

I stared at the pizza on my plate, my hands resting on the table alongside. My existence had been everything but fulfilling. Lonely, even though I surrounded myself with godly people from church. Having gone God's route, there was no allowance for what my flesh wished for.

"It's the life I've chosen." I finally gave what I could.

"Because it's what your grandfathers and parents wanted or because you felt drawn to traipse down a path that holds no sure light at the end of the tunnel?"

He'd been around enough to know the answer to that one himself. Jacob and I had been hounded to go into the ministry for as long as I could remember, and Aiden had witnessed more than one attempt at persuasion from Gramps.

"Sorry," he muttered when I didn't reply. "Shannon always said I couldn't just let things lie."

"It's okay," I stated quietly, thankful my groin had gone back to its usual numb, limp state over his inquiry into my privacy. "What about you?"

"What about me?"

"Did you find a church out in California?"

"Fuck, no," he answered and quickly cleared his throat as though uncomfortable for having cursed in front of a pastor.

"Swearing doesn't bother me," I told him the truth. God knew such words rang through my head often enough. I just chose to not release them into the air. "How did you spend your spare time?"

"The last six months it's been at the gym."

That wasn't something I would have had to guess at. His T-shirt was as tight as the one he'd had on earlier and just as revealing when it came to what lay beneath the cotton.

Thick muscle I wanted to sink my teeth into. Popping veins my tongue drooled to trace.

I tore my attention off a body honed to entice

lustful thoughts to a celibate man like myself. "My friend Aaron works at a gym right around the corner if you're looking to join one," I said.

My mind went to Aaron's boyfriend Ezra who I'd been blessed with working alongside for a few months before he left the church—for loving a man. Zeke, another friend, had done the same and married Levi.

All four had found happiness in their supposed sin while I struggled to discover joy in the Lord.

Loneliness, the faithful bitch, settled down over my shoulders again, and I bowed beneath the weight of helplessness—the truth of what my choices in life had left me with.

Not a whole lot.

I should have found fulfillment in obeying God's commands and living in a way that was pleasing in His sight.

But I didn't.

"Do you ever work out there?" Aiden asked, and I shook my head.

"Martin's," I said, my voice wanting to break. "It's two blocks from here."

"We ought to work out together sometime."

I snapped my head side to side. No way in hell could I go to a gym with Aiden and not stare at him as he sweated and grunted to lift weights.

Just like that, the feeling of solitariness dissipated as lust rushed back in. Aiden's gaze seared my face, and my stomach fluttered. "How about that movie?" I said, getting up from the table without having finished my pizza.

———

Sitting on my couch and hanging out wasn't like old times, unfortunately. Aiden and I were no longer young kids without a care in the world. We'd lived. Learned. He'd loved. Longing and the need for a pillow on my lap carried over from my childhood, but no sense of hopefulness resided inside me like back then.

Depression had always knocked on my doorstep but worsened with age.

I eyed Aiden in my periphery as I'd done for years, everything physically about him calling to me. Warmth seemed to radiate off him even though a couch cushion separated us. Each shift of his body made me hyperaware of his presence. His laughter at young Han Solo's sense of humor lightened my chest, and the curses he let out over whatever tension transpired on the screen had me smiling.

Happiness, I realized as the movie drew to a close. That was the emotion Aiden brought back to my life outside my family, and I hadn't realized how much I'd craved it.

Thankfully, my groin behaved toward the end of the movie, and I managed to walk Aiden into the kitchen as he prepared to head out.

Melancholy waited, I didn't doubt, and I had the sudden urge to keep him there, to stall his leaving for as long as possible.

But what to say? What excuse could I use to keep the man at my apartment when he had unpacking to do and a bed to collapse on?

Forcing my thoughts off anything mattress-related, I acted on a whim and dug into my kitchen's junk drawer.

"Here." I held out the spare key to my place.

"What's this for?" he asked but opened his hand.

I dropped the gift onto his palm without touching his skin. "Like old times," I went with and shrugged, trying not to focus on his thick chest I wanted to suck until bruised. "Mi casa and all that... if you need anything."

Aiden ruffled my hair, but unlike when I'd been a kid, I didn't jerk away or glare. I stayed still, my eyelids fluttering shut at his touch. If leaning into his hand and purring like a cat wouldn't have raised his eyebrows or made him think I was weird, I'd have gone for it.

I soaked in his petting, my insides creating the whirring sound I wouldn't allow my lips to betray.

"Thanks for tonight, Jed," Aiden stated quietly, giving my hair one last tug.

I nodded, swallowing hard as he walked out the door, leaving me alone.

He'd called me Jed.

A smile cracked through the tears welling in my eyes.

4

AIDEN

Hanging with Jacob's brother relaxed one part of me and confused the fuck out of another. Being with him gave me that sense of home I'd been missing out in California, the comfortable feeling of rightness I'd always had around his family.

But something more lay beneath the surface of an old friendship found again.

I'd felt the tension from Jed, and while I hated that my presence stirred supposed sinful thoughts in his head, I reveled in knowing why he held that pillow in his lap.

Memories had crashed through me all night long of his behavior as a teenager. His sneaking around, side-eyeing me all the damn time, flushed face if I gave him my full attention. The boners he'd popped around me and tried to hide.

Sadist.

I smirked at my bedroom ceiling, my hands laced behind my head. Why did I enjoy making him uncomfortable? As an eighteen-year-old, I'd gotten a kick out of walking around the Simpson house half-dressed, preening beneath his not-so-covert glances.

Jed's conscience, what he probably considered to be the Holy Spirit, probably suggested he look the other way, but he still desired an eyeful.

And I wanted to give it to him.

My dick tented the sheet draped over my hips—morning wood, I told myself as the sun rose beyond my bedroom's window.

I'm not gay.

I wrapped my fist around my length and tugged a bit, thankful as fuck my libido seemed normal for the first time in months.

I'd gotten back to my apartment the night before, unconcerned about the boxes or the chore of getting settled in ahead of me. Details could wait, I'd realized. I still had a life to live.

A new start...I could do whatever the fuck I wanted.

Jed.

His big brown eyes popped into my memory, the long lashes. Flushed cheeks. The hard swallows and parted lips he couldn't seem to help around me, same as when he'd been a kid.

My dick leaked while I fisted myself, and I

groaned at the unusual sensation of need firming my balls up against my body.

I didn't question what the hell was wrong with me. I just allowed nature to have its way as tension coiled in my groin with every stroke of my hand down over my length, taking me to the edge fast as hell.

My mind wandered, and I let it. Those damn fluffy socks of Jed's that shouldn't have had me thinking about what his feet looked like. If his toes were ticklish.

The tight ass beneath his sweats, rounded globes that would fit in my palms.

Would he like my hands on him?

Would he even allow any type of affection if I wanted to give it to him?

Would he enjoy watching the slick head of my dick thrusting up through my fist?

"Oh, fuck." My jaw clenched, and a ribbon of cum shot clear to my chest. "Shit." I lifted my head off my pillow and eyed my pulsing dick. Breathing heavily through my nose, I imagined Jed staring as I painted my abs with sticky white.

Two more spurts joined those already smeared on my skin, one last bit of spunk dribbling down over my fingers as I milked my balls empty.

I didn't doubt he'd whimper over the sight I made. Maybe even come in his boxers without a single touch.

Let me lick you clean.

"Fuck." A shudder rippled over me as I pushed away the thought of what he might say. While I should have been relaxed, sated, and rested, energy rippled through my body, keeping me wound tight.

I needed the goddamn gym to get my mind over what it was about Jed that made me shoot my load like that. Blowing off steam would ease whatever it was stirring my insides. A friend of Jed's and two blocks away from home? Couldn't ask for much more.

After a hot shower and a cup of coffee later, I made my way to Martin's. The gym was nicer than most I'd been in. Smelled like cleaning supplies— but subtle—rather than sweat and body odor.

A dark-haired gym rat stood behind the counter, his tight-as-fuck T-shirt revealing a stacked upper body even a straight guy could appreciate.

Aaron, his name tag read, just as I'd been hoping.

I grinned and stuck out my hand. "Name's Aiden —Jed suggested I come check the gym out."

"Pastor Jed?" Aaron asked, clasping my hand and giving me a quick once-over.

Chuckling at the title I couldn't wrap my head around even though it fit the kid I'd known, I nodded. "He's a childhood friend. I just moved back here from California."

"Welcome home."

Home. The word sounded and felt right after my dinner date with Jed. My smile stretched, but I didn't read into my feelings too much.

"So where do I sign up?" I asked, glancing around. Bikes, row machines, stair climbers, and enough weights and benches to keep plenty of people busy littered the large area even though the place already buzzed with energy from those working out.

Aaron ran me through the membership information, and I handed over cash for a six-month stint since it gave a nice discount.

I followed him back to the locker rooms for a quick tour.

A couple of guys were changing, and Aaron greeted a few by name and introduced me. We exchanged the usual head tips and "What's up?" bullshit macho guys usually did, and my focus remained above the chest since two stood in nothing but skin.

While I was tall and wide, I tended to tower over most—Aaron included even though the man was jacked. A giant strode from the showers, a towel slung low on his trim hips, for the first time in years making me feel...small.

"Michael," Aaron said, "this is Aiden."

Rarely did a person intimidate me, but Michael was a goddamn beast. I shook his hand, receiving another once-over from him that swelled my chest even though his gaze lingered long enough to make guessing his sexual orientation easy.

"Don't get any ideas," Aaron said, slapping the back of his hand against Michael's thick chest. "He's Pastor Jed's friend."

Michael chuckled at Aaron, not seeming the least bit embarrassed by getting caught checking me out. "Pastors can be persuaded to indulge—you would know, Aaron. Or has that sexy silver fox of yours finally realized he can do better?"

He.

Jed had gay friends.

Aaron grinned while shaking his head at Michael. "Asshole." No anger or annoyance laced the word, and I wondered over their relationship.

He headed back toward the gym. I followed, feeling Michael's gaze on me every step of the way.

I didn't hate the attention but reminded myself I wasn't gay.

"My partner Ezra used to be a pastor," Aaron explained once we left Michael behind.

So there's hope for swaying Jed—

I coughed, a curse cutting off the thought. I had no intention of being anything more than a friend to Jacob's little brother.

Telling myself it was just the interest he showed me that got my engine running, I focused on wearing my ass out.

But I lied. Michael's blatant lust hadn't done jack

shit for my dick, and I couldn't beat my body down enough to rest.

I got home after a killer workout, unpacked all my shit, and still had energy to spare. Boredom set in, so I doodled a little, wasting away time.

My cell buzzed, and I grinned to find my mom's caller ID pic of her with her tongue sticking out and eyes crossed. She and Dad had visited me in California the summer before and we'd had too much fun at my favorite bar.

"Hey, lady," I said in greeting, kicking back onto my couch with a bottle of water.

"How's my only son?" she asked as she always did. "All settled in?"

"Good and somewhat. I still have a few things to get organized."

"And the new apartment?"

I glanced around the living area that looked like a bachelor pad without a single bit of personality. "It's a place to crash—you'll never guess who lives across the hall. Jacob's brother, Jed."

"You're kidding."

"Nope." A sip of coolness slid down my throat.

"Is that poor boy still in love with you?"

I choked and coughed, sitting up again to clear the water from the wrong tube. "What?"

"I know you're hurting after the divorce, but don't you dare take advantage of him."

"Mom!"

"I'm serious, Aiden McNelis. He's too good to be your rebound. Find someone else to boost back up your self-esteem that poisonous bitch ripped to shreds."

I hadn't told my parents the truth of what had happened with Shannon, but obviously my mom had seen more than I realized.

A lot more.

"I'm not into guys, Mom," I stated after too long of a pause, hoping to put the conversation to rest.

"Hmm."

An emitted sound of disagreement.

"I'm *not*." I shifted on my couch—and grimaced at the realization that my second head had other thoughts.

"And Shannon?"

My dick wilted like a dead flower.

"She's in my past, and I'm ready to start my life over again."

"I know you are. Just...make good choices, okay?"

"When have I done anything but?"

"Getting shit faced with your old mother and taking silly photos wasn't exactly smart."

I grinned. "Fun as hell, though."

"That it was." Her tone revealed she flashed the smile I'd inherited. "We'll see you for dinner this weekend, right?"

"Wouldn't miss it for the world."

"I'll give Dad smooches for you."

"You do that," I said, chuckling.

I hung up a minute later, still grinning, but boredom overtook me again.

Around four, I grabbed the slice of leftover pizza Jed had sent home with me and realized I'd left my last beer in his fridge.

Mouth stuffed full, I shot him a text, hoping he'd see it sooner than later. **Mind if I go into your apartment and grab that beer I left last night?**

Jed's reply came through within seconds. **Go right ahead.**

Me: **Thanks, neighbor!**

He sent a smiley face that brought back my grin.

Letting myself into his place kind of made me feel like a creep, and I glanced around the tidy apartment before heading into the kitchen. Cold can in my hand, I turned and cracked it open, chasing down the pizza I'd inhaled.

Bland colors on the walls, I noted what I hadn't the night before. No pictures or anything personal littered the living room, same as my place—and he'd lived there for years. A throw blanket lay folded on the back of the couch, and the only piece of artwork adorning the walls was a painting of the sky with beams of sunlight filtering down through the clouds.

God, I expected Jed thought of while gazing at it.

A source of heat and energy to me.

For how Jed adored his sci-fi shit, I'd expected some movie paraphernalia on the walls or decorating his lone bookshelf like back when he'd lived at his parents, but nope.

Nothing.

My feet took me farther into his home, and I paused by his open bedroom door he'd closed the night before. Inside, I found where he hid his true self. Papers, notebooks, and an old laptop covered in X-wing fighter stickers sat atop the desk tucked in the corner.

A twin-sized Star Wars comforter draped over his double bed, worn from use.

I snorted a laugh, shaking my head even though I wasn't surprised. The framed movie poster of *A New Hope* hung above, again expected since he'd had the same one when he'd been a kid. But the baby Yoda stuffed animal on his dresser? My eyebrows popped up.

His bedstand caught my attention, intensifying my creep factor—but that didn't stop me from striding across his room and pulling the drawer open.

My grin spread at the same time my dick woke fully the fuck up. "Oh, Jed. You naughty, naughty boy."

Lube. Butt plugs. Dildos. A fucking Fleshlight—an ass, not a make-believe pussy.

"Shit." I picked up that last toy, all the blood in my body rushing to my groin. I imagined Jed working that thing over his dick, the squelching noises of lube stuffing in the tight, pink hole.

But the other toys...he fantasized about taking it up the ass too.

Why the fuck did the fact he would bend both ways make my hole clench and balls tighten?

"The fuck, man." I scrubbed a hand down over my face and put Jed's toy back, but something caught my eye, keeping me from firmly shutting the drawer.

I pulled my old sketchbook from beneath Jed's toys, turning it over in my hands. I'd had dozens of the doodle-covered notebooks when I'd been younger—I hadn't even realized I missed one.

He'd stolen it from me.

"That little shit!" I chuckled, curious about what else he might have snagged of mine from all those years ago. Keepsakes of his crush? A love for my drawings? Regardless of his reasons, a sense of satisfaction swelled inside of me.

My cell dinged in my pocket, causing adrenaline to shoot through my blood and my heart to race. Feeling like I'd been caught with my hand in the cookie jar, I shoved the book back where it'd been hidden, quietly shut the drawer, and swiped the screen to life.

Jed: **Did you find what you were looking for?**

"Christ." I barked a laugh, wondering why the fuck he hadn't just asked if I'd gotten my goddamn beer. His text? Yeah. It made my head spin, same as the short conversation I'd had with Mom.

I'd found more than I knew what to do with, that was for damn sure.

Yeah, I typed out and hit send.

Jed: **I'm going to stop by Sully's for cheesesteaks on my way home tonight. Do you want one?**

I began typing the first line that came to mind, knowing he would smile. **Want one, I do.**

Jed replied with an eye roll then laughter emoji, letting me know he got my Yoda imitation like I'd expected he would. **I'll be home in about an hour and bring yours over to you.**

Me: **Another date?**

I included one of those googly eye, tongue sticking out emojis so he wouldn't take me too seriously.

Jed's reply was a long time in coming, and I stood back inside my own kitchen before my cell dinged again. **Sure.**

Fluttery wings woke in my guts, making a mess of my head—but not my dick. He at least knew what he wanted.

So, I gave my balls the release they ached for, telling myself after shooting a shit ton of spunk all over my abs again that I seriously needed to go pick up a woman and get laid.

5

———

JED

Another date with Aiden.

I slid my cell back in my suit coat pocket. "Sorry about that."

"I can't imagine having an electronic leash is as pleasant as all you youngsters seem to think," Mr. Williams grumbled.

I eyed the old man propped up with pillows in his bed, wondering how he'd held onto life as long as he had. Ninety-seven and kicking it up until the previous two weeks when he'd had to be placed in a nursing home due to a fall and a broken hip.

Like quite a few of those I visited along the hall-ways, no family came to ease his loneliness, so I'd added him to my must-see list on Tuesday afternoons.

"Way back when it was dial-up and handwritten

letters, huh?" I asked even though I knew the answer. There wasn't much better than listening to the older folks reminisce about days gone past. And there wasn't a more enjoyable response I received for volunteering than seeing their eyes go misty with memories and smiles lighting their faces.

"We didn't even have dial-up when I was a kid," Mr. Williams said, his tone firm and strong for his age.

I settled forward, elbows on my knees, but for the first time in all my years appreciating my hours spent at the nursing home, I struggled to focus on the words shared with me.

Aiden had occupied my thoughts all day while in my office at the church and the distraction of him had carried over to my hour of volunteer work. I'd been visiting invalids at Blackstone Senior Living since entering the ministry, and I found more joy in sitting with them than my pastoral duties at Simply Grace.

While private with my own life, I thoroughly enjoyed hearing about others'.

Mr. Williams hadn't mentioned a wife and children or even grandchildren, but I'd realized if you got people talking long enough, you would hear about those they would leave behind.

"Have you ever been in love?"

I blinked at the question, refocusing my mind on

the present and the old man peering at me. *Aiden.* "I...ah, no. Not really."

"I found the love of my life on the day I turned seventeen." Mr. Williams's eyelids closed, and I too settled back to enjoy the story. "It was also the first day of our senior year in school. Eyes dark as coffee, hair the color of wheat. Mouth a little too wide, and a snaggled front tooth I thought was adorable."

Mr. Williams went quiet for a few minutes, and I imagined him reliving that moment in time. He seemed the confident type who would be drawn to the wallflower, a timid girl who needed a knight in shining armor.

"He was beautiful and everything I hadn't realized I'd wanted until that moment."

He.

I sat forward once more, my heart rate kicking up the slightest bit. "What was his name?" I dared to ask since I thought perhaps he'd misspoken the pronoun.

"Jonathan."

Nope. I'd gotten it right. A soft smile crept over my face.

"I suppose as a pastor you think I'm a heathen for loving and living with a man for seventy-three years." Mr. Williams opened his eyes and met my stare, a hint of stubbornness lifting his chin.

"It's not my place to judge," I stated kindly what I always did when faced with such questions.

Mr. Williams grunted and tilted his head away again, once more enjoying the darkness behind closed eyes. "Seventy-three years, and cancer took him from me. I couldn't bear being alone. We had no children—homosexuals couldn't adopt back in the day—and both our parents and siblings had shunned us when they'd learned the two young roommates were more than best friends."

An ache pinged through my chest, the same fear I felt whenever I thought of my family learning of my sexual preference for Aiden.

"I held a gun to my head on the day I buried him."

His words hit me like a punch to my chest. I waited, but Mr. Williams didn't elaborate.

"What stopped you?" I asked quietly.

"The fear of no afterlife, thinking that I wouldn't be able to remember our love once my heart stopped beating." A tear slid down his cheek.

He'd chosen memories over darkness.

Even if they caused immeasurable grief.

I covered Mr. Williams's hand with my own, squeezing, but I didn't have any words to offer comfort. Only questions that had battered my brain almost daily since first seeing Aiden.

"If you had to go back to that day you met Jonathan," I finally decided to speak, "would you do things differently knowing the end result of your family setting you aside for love you had no control over?"

"No." He didn't hesitate to answer. "Blood will never trump sharing a life with the person fate intended for you."

To have such confidence, such a lack of fear—but his had come after years of learning.

My crush on Aiden had been one-sided since the age of fourteen, and stepping outside all I'd known to seek out such a love Mr. Williams and Jonathan had enjoyed would only land me in heartache.

But what if it didn't?

What if Aiden held secret feelings for me as well? Would a relationship be worth pursuing? Did I care for him enough to let my family go in the hopes he would fill the gaping hole losing them would create in my life?

"You must have loved him very much," I stated, wanting to commend Mr. Williams for taking that chance.

"Always."

My throat tightened at the firm assurance in his answer. "Tell me about him?" I managed to croak out my request, hoping speaking of his love would bring Mr. William the comfort I never could as a mere stranger.

He eyed me once more. "You want to hear about two gay lovers who shared a bed for almost three-quarters of a century?"

"Please."

And I didn't doubt I would deal with envy over every story he recounted.

———

I waited in line at Sully's for the cheesesteak order I had called in after leaving the nursing home, my heart full and throat still tight.

Mr. Williams had zero regrets about the choices he'd made.

He'd lost his family.

He'd lost friends.

He'd lost out on a lot of rights most people of my era forgot to appreciate.

All because of love, the kind that bound hearts together regardless of time or space.

Mr. Williams had admitted to being ready for whatever lay beyond—an afterlife with Jonathan or peaceful quiet. He'd come to rest in his heart that they'd had a full life, but memories no longer sustained him.

I couldn't imagine such a love, but I understood the yearning for what was outside your reach.

My heart ached for it.

"Order for Simpson!" the man behind the counter called out, and I forced aside my depressing thoughts.

I had a date to look forward to even if it wasn't

the kind my flesh would have preferred. There would be no snuggling on the couch after finishing our meal, no kissing and touching, no fulfilling the desire that had kept me awake long into the night.

At least I hadn't woken up with sticky boxers.

With every mile slipping behind my car, my nervousness heightened. The memory of wide shoulders and glinting hazel eyes ramped me up as it'd done all day, and until I climbed the stairs rather than taking the elevator to our floor—get that exercise in and shed the worries of the day—my heart raced. Sweat trickled down my spine.

If I'd had a free hand, I would have yanked my tie loose so I could draw enough oxygen into my lungs to stop me from passing out.

I hadn't been able to say no to Aiden's teasing suggestion of a date. The "sure" I'd sent didn't let on to my excitement, but why did he even use that word? I knew from our short time the night before that he'd become more liberal than the family he'd left behind.

He claimed his ex hadn't liked how he poked for information, but he'd always been that way. Nosey— annoying to someone secretive like me.

Had he guessed at my crush on him?

Or perhaps, he *was* bi and possibly interested in more than friendship with me. My heart raced at the idea. What better way to prod a private person than drop hints rather than confront and clam a mouth up?

I chewed on the inside of my lip, slightly out of breath by the time I reached the third floor.

No matter Aiden's reasoning, I needed to hide my feelings for him. Giving him the truth of my longing, allowing him to know he tempted me as no person ever had, would only end in disaster.

For my family.

My heart.

Aiden had married a woman, and I couldn't hope that his preferences had gone toward skinny men who had an outie rather than an innie between their thighs.

I snorted, shaking my head.

Thirty-four, and I sometimes thought like a kid.

Weirdo.

I still had my old Star Wars comforter from when I'd turned twelve. Could I be any more pitiful?

My old friend depression arrived as I ambled down the hallway, but she did nothing to slow my thrumming pulse.

Not for the first time, I wished God would take the affliction of wanting Aiden from me. Fill me with the desire for a woman, softer flesh that smelled of flowers and sweetness rather than musk and citrus.

Please, God.

I stood in front of Aiden's door, my grip on the bag containing his dinner tighter than necessary.

Perhaps a quick shower and jerk-off would allow me to relax and enjoy eating a cheesesteak with my friend.

Inhaling until it hurt, I rapped my knuckles against his door and waited. Lightheaded and turned on. Scared as hell. Heat rose to my face no matter how much I tried to remain calm.

I wasn't just pitiful, but a hot mess too.

6

AIDEN

Jed showed up at my door still dressed in his church clothes. His stare on my bare chest, he shoved the bag with our cheesesteaks at me. His tongue flicked over his lower lip, twinging life through my groin.

Not. Gay.

"Here." He sounded breathless. "I'm going to go get changed."

Smirking at the pink on his cheeks, I took the bag, flexing my pecs and making sure my fingers brushed his.

His gulped and spun around, his tight ass hurrying across the short hallway. I chuckled long after he hid himself from my lingering gaze.

Christ, did I love him crushing on me. Swelled my ego and my dick I thought I'd milked dry. Something drew me to him physically, but fuck if I knew what it was.

I thought about Aaron and his partner Ezra who had stopped by the gym while I'd been working out that morning. The two were madly in love, handsy with each other behind the desk but not in a trashy way. It was like they were extensions of one another, the magnetism between them almost tangible.

So damn in love, I'd been a little envious of how their gazes held while conversing.

I'd explained that away by what I'd been through the previous six months with the woman I'd believed had been my person.

Shoving aside memories of Shannon, I pulled out a couple of plates and set my small square table for my not-really date with Jed. Just a couple of guys hanging out and shooting the shit.

Why I'd suggested a date again, I didn't know.

Because Jed's attention soothes my bruised ego.

Perhaps Mom's assumption I'd go for Jed as a self-esteem boosting rebound hadn't been too far off the mark.

"Not gay," I reminded myself with a firm tone.

A timid knock announced my visitor and slid a shot of adrenaline through my system.

I opened the door, that strangeness slithering down my spine to tingle my balls.

Jed had taken a quick shower, the dark hair atop his head tousled and still damp. Like the night before, he wore a pair of sweats, a T-shirt, and a pair of fluffy socks—with Boba Fett on them.

Again, he stared at my chest, but I stepped out of his way, biting back a grin.

The ego boost?

I let it roll through me, and fuck, was it ever a high. I felt...alive again.

"Cute socks."

"Shut up," he muttered while tearing his focus off my body, my new favorite shade highlighting his cheekbones. "They're comfortable."

"They're also *you*," I added, not wanting to embarrass him or make him feel like a kid.

He scooted around me into my apartment, taking care to keep from touching me.

I shut the door, locking us in. "I love that you haven't put aside that part of my Padawan."

Jed pulled up in the kitchen and gave me his eyes for all of three seconds, his quick inquisitive stare not allowing me a full read of what he thought. "I'm pitiful. Weird."

"The fuck you are," I stated, my grin gone as he sat at the table. "There's nothing weird about enjoying the good parts of the entertainment industry."

Adult entertainment.

I wondered over that laptop on Jed's desk and half wanted to kick myself for not snooping around a little bit more and learning how deeply Jed's lust for dick went.

Clearing my throat, I attempted to shake my thoughts loose.

"So, tell me about your day," I said, taking a chair at my table and forcing my attention on anything but the idea of Jed watching guys get off with each other. In each other. Mouths, ass...

Fuck.

Jed slid onto the other seat and busied himself with his wrapped cheesesteak while I fought against my dick's twitching. "It was a long day. Boring as heck."

"Sounds like being a pastor is fulfilling." I couldn't help but poke and make him squirm.

That earned me another three-second stare. "I'll admit," he said quietly, turning his focus once more to his dinner, "my choice of profession isn't ideal."

"Profession," I repeated. "Not a *calling*?" I repeated what I'd heard countless times over my early adult years spent sitting in front of a pulpit with the Simpson family.

Jed chewed, thinking so damn hard I could hear him over my own teeth tearing into my dinner. He wasn't one to share personal shit, I knew, but I couldn't help but dig.

"Fuck, that's good," I spoke around my mouthful. The West Coast didn't know jack shit about cheesesteaks.

"Sully's is the best."

"Mmm," I agreed and attempted to fill the hole in my stomach with the juicy steak and rich cheese in my hands.

"I never felt the calling." Much to my surprise, Jed went back to my question after a few minutes of quiet munching. He seemed the close-lipped sort, same as when he'd been younger.

I studied his downturned face, the slight furrow between his dark eyebrows. His hair had dried, hanging over his forehead, and I had the urge to stroke my fingers through it, tipping his head back to meet my gaze.

"Why'd you do it, then?" I asked, rather than giving in to the odd desire to put my hands on him.

He shrugged. "Because it was expected of me."

"And you've stuck to a godly life, haven't you?" I asked, remembering all I'd seen in his bedstand drawer earlier that afternoon.

"For the most part?" His reply sounded more like a question than a statement, and I expected he attempted to skirt lying outright.

He shifted on the chair, and I bit back a smirk, my blood thrumming like a kid playing tag with his friends. Fuck not poking. I enjoyed seeing him squirm, and he had it too bad for me to ignore me for the rest of his life.

"Are you a virgin?"

Jed's head jerked up, his eyes wide. "Wh-what?"

He gasped the word, and my lips curved upward even though I'd attempted to keep them flatlined.

"You know...virtuous. Unsullied. Pure in body as our old pastor used to preach about. Waiting for marriage—that sort of shit."

"That's none of your business," he snipped out, even the tips of his ears flushing.

The thought of him being untouched did some strange shit to my insides—and my dick. Curiosity over my swelling length lit inside me—I had to fucking know.

"Are. You. A. Virgin?" I asked again and tore off another bite of my dinner, waiting to see how his answer would affect my body.

His focus dropped to my mouth while I chewed, an adorable blank expression replacing the annoyance on his face.

More blood rushed to my groin, but I didn't question my reaction—just went with it.

"It's no big deal if you are," I said after swallowing. "Kinda cool, really."

All that sinewy muscle untasted by man or woman. His dick only having experienced his own fist—and that pink Fleshlight.

A shift to ease my discomfort from having my dick bent at the wrong angle jerked Jed's focus back to the last bit of steak still on his plate.

"Yes," he whispered, his face red as marinara sauce.

Fuck, his answer shouldn't have been as hot as it was. I shifted on my chair, trying for a discrete adjustment. Why the fuck was the truth of his purity such a fucking turn on? And why did I feel a sudden urge to dirty him up?

"Do you still like boys?" I heard myself ask—too damn late to take it back when his face went from red to white.

"N-no!" he sputtered, rubbing his hands down his thighs beneath the table and studying the partial cheesesteak still on his plate.

I'd definitely crossed a line.

"I don't care if you do," I hastened to say, shrugging with a nonchalance I felt in my mind but definitely not in my body. "I think people should be free to love whoever the fuck they want. That reminds me...I met Aaron this morning, and he and Ezra are so in love it's almost sickening."

Jed let out a heavy breath, relaxing the tension my personal questions had caused.

My intentional change of topic worked like a charm, thank fuck. If only I could get my dick to calm like I'd done with Jed.

"They are—and it is," he murmured, picking his cheesesteak back up with slender fingers.

He took a bite and licked a smear of grease from the corner of his mouth, the quick peek of pink tongue catching my gaze.

Virginal. Sweet and kind. Cute...no, *hot*, actually.

I rolled those adjectives around in my head while he finished his meal, allowing myself to see and finally understand the pull.

It was attraction I felt for Jacob's little brother, plain and simple. But not just for his untouched body I had an animalistic urge to filthy up. His softer nature drew me in, made me want to wrap my arms around him again and hold him until he realized he could trust me with his secrets.

A slow exhale leaked from my parted lips that would have preferred to be punched free from my lungs.

I was bi. Or, I was, at least for Jed.

What would he think if he knew the truth? Would he be interested in exploring the attraction between us?

Would I?

My dick sure as fuck was on board with the idea.

How would Jacob feel if I started dating his brother? And what about Jed's church?

I could imagine the shit that would hit the fan.

It wouldn't be pretty—but I couldn't stop the temptation to find out.

7

JED

I could feel Aiden's stare from across the table as I attempted to finish my dinner. While chewing, I agonized over what he thought about the very personal information I had admitted to even though I hated my life being put under scrutiny.

The only time I'd touched another human outside of platonic friendship was in my dreams, and even then, just Aiden. If he knew the truth, I wouldn't have been welcome at his table, and I couldn't stomach the thought of him pushing me away.

He might say a person ought to be allowed to love who they would, but he saw me as a kid, Jacob's little brother. Incestuous, I imagined he'd think of my desire for him, same as my family would.

Forbidden—and just downright *wrong*, same as

my burning lust to kiss and bite every inch of golden skin bared to me above the tabletop. Who sat down to dinner without a shirt?

I'd considered insisting he put one on when I'd come back after my shower to find him barely clothed, same as when I'd dropped off our dinner, but didn't want to embarrass him.

At least that was what I told myself.

I loved seeing all that skin, those furled brown nipples tempting my tongue, my teeth.

I struggled with unholy urges to mark his body, but his presence filled a huge void in my life I'd been struggling with for years, and I couldn't leave. My flesh wanted him as a lover and so much more, same as always, but the rest of me wished for friendship.

Someone I could lean on outside my parents.

Someone who wouldn't mind me calling or texting because he enjoyed talking to me.

Someone to spend time with.

"How was the gym this morning?" I asked, finally thinking I needed a life outside the church. Maybe I *could* handle having to hear him grunt while lifting.

I imagined his rasped voice letting out any type of guttural noise...*and* nope.

Definitely not.

"The place was great. Clean, it was. Full of eye candy."

I checked his face, sure he meant to goad me even while making a Yoda joke. "Imagine, I can."

He waggled his eyebrows, and I knew he set up to tease me. "All those *men* in skimpy shorts and tank tops—a delight to the senses."

And I could imagine hell on a normal gay man's libido. It was how his voice rasped the suggestion rather than the thought of other men that kicked my pulse up a notch.

I had to push back, considering the door he'd left open with his choice of words. The jerk deserved it for how he teased me as though hoping to pin down an answer to what he'd asked about my sexuality. "Men, huh? Have you given up your love of the fairer sex?"

His focus slipped to my mouth, and he was the one to flit his attention away.

Aiden shifted on his chair, clearing his throat, and I stared, sure I misread his reaction. "I never said guys didn't do it for me."

My jaw went unhinged, and I blinked a few times before snapping it shut.

Did he just...seriously?

I shook my head even as my heart raced. "But you haven't...you...never mind."

"Say it."

I chewed the inside of my lip.

"Jed." His husky tone meant business and shot a zing of lust through my groin.

"Fine," I gave in because my curiosity would keep me up all hours of the night otherwise with a hope it had no right to. "You only ever dated girls. You married a woman."

"Biggest damn mistake of my life too," Aiden muttered, getting up and grabbing a beer from his fridge. "Want one?"

"You know I don't."

"I'm going to sway you to the dark side," Aiden said with a wink before sitting back down.

"I will never use the Force for evil."

He snorted on a laugh, almost spewing beer across the table while I grinned. "This is nice, Jed." His slow smile fluttered my belly, and I had to look away.

"It is."

Aiden reached over the table and gave my shoulder one of the bro slaps I'd always envied others sharing.

Warmth spread through me beyond sexual want.

"I haven't seen the last three Star Wars movies, the ones with that Rey girl."

"You haven't?" I asked, straightening up as excitement brewed my insides.

"You have those on Blu-Ray too?"

He'd teased me the night before about being possessive rather than the streaming type when it came to owning movies.

"Are you really asking me that?" I let out a genuine laugh for the first time in months.

"So who's hotter—Rey or Kylo?"

Jerk.

Heat filled my face. How Aiden managed to get under my skin so easily should've been worrisome, but I didn't fear him, his intentions, or why he probed me for personal information. He'd never been anything but kind to me, and after his confession about not being interested in women only, I expected I could trust him.

"Kylo." I decided to give him an actual peek into my private life. "Hands down."

"Think he'll sway *me* fully to the dark side?" Aiden's eyes twinkled in the way that always made me hard.

I realized I held his gaze longer than I ever had. My smile spread. "His voice alone can entice the straightest man to give into temptation."

Aiden's eyes glinted as he popped the last of his dinner into his mouth. "We'll see about that, Padawan," he spoke around his food.

A test of sorts?

Definitely a bet...I wondered where Aiden's mind was at.

Not that I truly cared about his sexuality or what it meant to me, I told myself.

Lies.

I lusted to know if the idea of dick turned him on...if he'd wondered what my lips tasted like when

I caught him staring at them. If he would enjoy my teeth scraping across his chest, marking him up.

But I'd made my bed fresh out of high school, and I couldn't fathom a life beyond what I had for sixteen years. It was all I'd known, the foundation I'd built everything upon.

Same as my loved ones.

Mr. Williams had said he'd choose Jonathan over his family every day for what they'd shared, but he'd never been a religious person.

I doubted I could do the same.

———

Renee, the secretary Pastor Welker and I shared, stuck her head into my office a little before noon the next day. "I'm heading over to the cafe for some lunch. Do you want anything?"

I smiled up at the woman who'd been Mom's best friend for as long as I could remember and could gossip with the best of them. "I brought half a cheesesteak leftover from last night's dinner, but thanks."

"Your mom told me Jacob's friend Aiden came back home."

Keeping my focus on Renee didn't come easy when I wanted to glance away to hide my feelings toward him. "He has, yes."

"Well, I hope he decides to become a part of our

church again. He was always so respectful and level-headed to your brother's wildness."

"Jacob certainly was that," I said with a grin, remembering how many times he'd lost privileges for his disobedience while I'd sat in silence and learned from his mistakes.

"It's such a blessing to see how your brother has grown in the Lord," Renee said. "Having him as the day school's principal these past couple of years has definitely boosted the student numbers and attitudes. I think it's helped that he sowed his oats as a kid. It's made him more empathetic. I've even heard a few of the teachers discussing how much easier he is to work beneath than Mr. Foss."

I nodded. We kids had called the dinosaur Mr. Foss-il even back when I'd been a kid, and he had overseen the day school since its beginning in the seventies.

"Are you sure you don't want anything? Tea? Coffee?"

"How about one of those white chocolate chunk cookies?" I suggested since I knew how much joy she got from bringing me food.

A mother at heart even though she'd never been blessed with a child of her own.

Renee winked. "You got it."

"Thanks!" I called after her, and she fluttered her fingers at me before shutting my office door.

I still smiled a few minutes later, thinking about

Mr. Foss suspending Jacob and Aiden because they'd put plastic wrap over the teacher lounge's toilet. Of course, Aiden wouldn't have come up with the idea. I'd always known it'd been Jacob's fault.

My office door swept inward without a knock, dissolving my smile.

Pastor Welker strode forward as though he owned the place—which he kind of did, his lips in a grim line. He quietly shut the door and sat across from me, hands folding over his opened suit coat.

"How long have you known Renee's husband?" he asked without a hello, good morning, or how are things going.

Well, good morning and afternoon to you too, I muttered in my mind.

I kept my face blank as I'd always been able to do —except for around Aiden. "Since I was a child. Is there a problem?"

He inhaled noisily as though steeling himself to deliver the worst news possible. Knowing the man's penchant for a bit of drama, I didn't start counting eggs of anxiety. One had to let them hatch from his mouth first.

"Have you seen him on the streets around your apartment complex?"

A frown dented my brow. "No."

"You know of the adult store across from that ungodly gym?"

Martin's—yes, I was aware of both places, actually.

"The one that breeds homosexuality?" Pastor Welker added before I answered.

I cleared my throat, fighting not to shift on my chair. "I believe so, yes."

"Aaron Weston works there. Ezra's partner." Welker's words snipped out, the bitterness in his eyes screaming homophobia.

My insides twisted, but I sat silent, waiting, tension rippling through my muscles to the point I wanted to vomit.

"Mr. Bowers happened to be driving by yesterday and saw Renee's husband enter that adult store."

It took me a few seconds to process the fact the church's treasurer had seen one of the members going into a store that sold more than just porn, whips, and chains.

And what did it matter how kinky a couple enjoyed being?

"The marriage bed is sacred," I finally decided on, and Pastor Welker's gaze narrowed, his eyes like daggers. Of course, I'd choose the wrong thing to remind him of. He didn't need to be schooled in God's word even if he sometimes manipulated the scripture for his own benefit.

Like being "God's man" and having been given his sermons directly from the Lord's mouth.

God hadn't ever spoken out loud to anyone in

recent times that I knew of. Hell, I'd never even heard of another pastor claiming such a thing.

"Be that as it may, what the members choose to do in public reflects on Simply Grace Church," Pastor Welker stated. "It reflects on me as their spiritual guide. And even on you as my right-hand man."

A snort rose at those last three words, but I held it in. Pastor Welker didn't require anyone at his side. His arrogance and pride in God's calling kept him on his own two feet without any problems.

I was nothing more than an extension of his office to fulfill duties he couldn't be bothered with. Visiting the sick. Sitting with the invalids. Offering empathy and encouragement to the hurting. And while I excelled at and enjoyed those tasks, I didn't feel needed or the least bit appreciated.

"Have you spoken with him?" I asked, wondering why he and Mr. Bowers hadn't just gone to Renee's husband like the Bible commanded to do if one of your brothers faltered. Why haul in yet another party—me—into the supposed problem?

"Not yet, no." Pastor Welker stood, smoothing down his striped tie over a belly that had begun to bulge since the year before. "I wanted to bring it to your attention since you live close by to that sinful area of town. You will be my eyes and ears, Pastor Jed, and report back any further evidence of misconduct."

Misconduct.

Yet another snort rose from my lungs that I barely cut off. I nodded even though I had zero intention of doing any such thing. If Renee and her husband were into ropes, floggers, or even pegging, what did it matter to me?

More power to them, and I hoped they enjoyed the hell out of their relationship until death parted them.

Envy snaked down through me at the thought of having such an open, loving relationship where no judgment resided, simply acceptance and mutual appreciation.

Pastor Welker strode from of my office as easily as he'd come in.

"Pastor Welker!" Renee greeted him in our shared reception area beyond my office. "I hadn't realized you'd come back already. I was just at the cafe, but can I get you some tea? Coffee?"

"You are such a sweetheart, Renee," Pastor Welker stated with a smooth, kind voice before my office door shut behind him.

I could imagine the smile he'd given her, the one that in the world outside the church would have at one time gotten him into women's panties without question.

My frown returned, and I let out a heavy exhale, trying to cleanse my mind, my thoughts.

Less than an ideal job, indeed—I considered the words I'd used about my choice with Aiden.

It wouldn't have been as bad if the man I'd submitted myself to didn't preach one thing and do another.

There was no end of gossip around the many offices of the church, about everyone but him though. While I tended to avoid whispers whenever possible, I expected the latest drama would include me whether I wanted it to or not.

But I refused to discuss Renee and her husband's sex life with Mom because she would only approach her best friend with the information, and I could imagine what kind of shit would get stirred up afterward.

"Nope," I muttered to myself, grabbing my bagged lunch and deciding to head outside to get some fresh air. "I'm not touching that one with a ten-foot pole."

Renee handed me my cookie as I made to escape outdoors, her smile sweet as pie—same as always, without a hint of underlying depression or sadness. God knew I saw enough of that in the mirror every day to recognize truth in a person's soul.

No, Renee was happy.

That sense of envy swept over me again, and I allowed myself a quiet moment beneath the sunshine to imagine such a life.

Waking in the morning to sleepy hazel eyes and mussed hair from a thorough loving the night before. Gentle kisses and murmured good mornings. Soft caresses over warm skin and hard muscle...

My body woke inside my slacks, and I allowed myself a few more minutes of fantastical bliss before returning to the real world.

8

AIDEN

I got to the gym before any other members on Thursday morning and headed to the locker room to drop off my bag.

Someone used the shower—Aaron, I knew, since he came in before opening to get his lifting done for the day.

I slipped my duffle off my shoulder, and a low groan echoed from the walled-off area of the locker room that held the shower stalls.

Shit.

Ezra had been in early with him the day before, and I wondered...

Another low groan.

"Oh, Ezzie..."

Aaron, and definitely his man worked him over in some way.

My conscience told me to quietly disappear,

giving them their privacy, but I couldn't make my feet move.

I imagined Ezra on his knees, their gazes locked while he sucked Aaron's dick. Tongued his balls. Played with his ass.

Blood began to drain to my groin, swelling me to half-mast as the two men morphed in my mind.

I saw my hands grasping Jed's hips as I drove into him with forceful thrusts. His pink hole stretching around my girth, attempting to suck me in every time I pulled back from his hot grasp.

I strained my ears like an absolute creep, the sounds of water and heavy breaths reaching me.

"Ah fuck." Aaron again. "I'm going to blow my load down your throat."

My eyelids slammed shut at the image of Jed on his knees, peering up at me, his gaze begging for my cum.

Ezra moaned a sound of approval.

"Thought you wanted my dick in your ass, Ezzie?"

Holy fucking shit.

I grabbed hold of my junk, inwardly cursing to keep my slit from leaking.

Why the fuck were the images in my head so fucking hot? Why did the dirty talk and groans make me so damn hard I couldn't breathe right?

My mind went back to Jed's laptop.

And what he might watch to get off.

Stop.

I gingerly set my bag on a bench and escaped the locker room. My mind overflowed, wondering if Aaron would give Ezra something to swallow or if the older preacher would bend over and offer his ass.

Or which Jed would prefer.

Which would *I* prefer if Jed offered?

"Shannon. Shannon." Muttering her name did the trick. My dick shriveled right the fuck up.

I stretched out a bit, forcing my mind off what went on in the locker room and the thoughts I'd had. The reminder of my ex, considering the workout ahead of me, and the plans for coffee I had with Jacob later that day kept me so occupied I got through the morning without popping another boner.

My old best friend was a busy man. Between his full-time job as principal of the school I'd attended my senior year after we'd moved to Philly, his wife Trish, and their twins, he had a lot on his plate.

I'd admit to feeling a little hurt, left out, since returning home. Not that I'd expected us to just jump right back into the closeness we'd shared before, but a part of me had hoped.

I wondered if seeing him so changed, hearing about all he'd accomplished and stories of Trish and his kids, would make things better or worse? Just the thought of listening to him brag, even if it *wasn't* bragging, twisted my guts.

Jacob had his shit together and got to enjoy the life he'd created for himself. While I lazed around and spent time at the gym—having to hear two guys doing...whatever the fuck they did in the locker room. I worked a few side jobs doing graphic design at night while agonizing over if I would start up another business.

Jealousy.

That was what I felt churning inside me.

I wanted what Jacob had, but the thought of another woman? I'd rather enjoy the non-drama, non-emotional attachment I expected Ezra and Aaron shared. Fuck knew two dudes wouldn't have all the same misunderstandings I'd endured.

No pettiness or gaslighting. And definitely no fucking hormonal bullshit every month.

The two men came out of the locker room a few minutes into my third set of curls. Hair wet, both flushed...Aaron had his hand on Ezra's lower back as they meandered toward the front desk.

Both waved at me when they glanced my way. Face hot, I went with the chin nod as if to ask how they were doing.

As if I *needed* to ask. Both of them smiling and appearing sated, it was obvious Ezra had bent over or Aaron had swallowed him down after getting his own dick sucked dry.

Again with the damn twinge of interest in my groin. Lips tight, I turned back to the mirrors I stood in front of and focused on popping the veins in my arms.

But I could see their reflection behind me.

Ezra followed Aaron around the desk, and they chatted for a few minutes, then shared a lingering kiss.

Chaste, but the first gay exchange of saliva I'd seen live instead of on-screen. Hot as fuck, and Christ, did my dick take notice.

Fully.

Same as listening to them go at it in the locker room while I'd imagined doing those things to Jed.

Shannon. Shannon.

Thank *fuck* her name was all it took to make me feel like a eunuch.

Unable to help myself, I stared at Aaron and Ezra until they broke apart. Both of them smiled, their lips moving again. After one last peck initiated by Aaron, his partner left with a wave.

Releasing a slow exhale, I focused on the reason I'd come to the gym. Blowing off steam and feeding my self-esteem.

Aaron ambled over a few minutes later, my dick still as limp as a wet dishrag, thank fuck. "How are things going?" he asked, watching my form.

"Good," I grunted and curled again.

His eyes on me while I lifted didn't get under my

skin like that giant, Michael's—Aaron didn't hold a shred of lust in his gaze. And why would he?

"Has Michael been bothering you?" Aaron asked.

The massive fucker had continued to flirt with me. I didn't hate it, but my body reacted differently than it did to thoughts of Jed.

"Nah. He's harmless." To my libido, anyway.

Aaron snorted, shoving his hands into his lounge pants pockets. "He's a horny fucker and relentless, so keep a watch out, okay?"

"Afraid he'll jump me in the showers?" I asked, smirking with a side-eye while placing the weights back on the rack.

Aaron cleared his throat and glanced toward the desk. "I, uh, saw your bag on the bench in the locker room."

Goddamnit. My face heated. "Yeah."

"Sorry if you...heard anything."

"It's all good, kid." I slapped his shoulder, trying for nonchalant even though my insides twisted up a bit over how my body had reacted. "Live it up while you can."

"Yeah." Aaron's sheepish grin dissolved, his blue eyes going dark with what seemed like grief. Jed had told me his dad had died a few weeks earlier. "Life's short and doesn't always offer second chances."

I shrugged, thinking of my boner killer. "And sometimes the first ones are bad enough you don't want to try again."

"Ezra did," Aaron stated quietly, a softer smile tipping up his lips, the haunted look in his eyes dissolving. "You know he was married before—to a woman. Ezra always thought he was straight, but he couldn't deny the pull between us."

"And if I had to guess, I'd say he's never been happier." A twinge of jealousy flared in my gut. A man attracted to another he'd connected to years earlier. Sounded similar enough I couldn't push the idea from my head that maybe I *wasn't* quite as straight as I'd always thought.

I eyed Aaron, the contentment on his face. "You've loved him for most of your life, Jed told me."

"I didn't realize what it was for years, but yeah. Never thought I'd see him again, never expected the chance to help set him free."

"I'd say you did a fine damn job," I stated quietly, once more remembering the noises they'd made in the shower. "You two are good together. Great, actually. Jed talks about you quite often."

"How's he doing?" Aaron took to studying my face, and I wondered how well he and Jed knew each other.

"Outwardly? I'd say he's fine."

"He hides a lot." Aaron didn't fish. Being who he was, I expected Aaron's gaydar pinged like fuck around Jed.

I wondered what he thought of *me*.

"He does," I agreed without giving any secrets

away. "But he's got a new friend in his life that has his best interests in heart."

"Do you?"

"Abso-fucking-lutely," I said, holding Aaron's steady stare. Let him see what he would—I had nothing to hide, and I expected the man wouldn't ever judge me for wanting what he and Ezra shared.

"Good." He slapped my shoulder. "Tell him I said hi."

"Will do."

Aaron moved off, checking in with other members who began to filter in with the sunrise.

Michael came in as I finished up, and he shot me a salacious wink from across the gym. I rolled my eyes back at him and shook my head. He pretended a heartfelt sigh that sagged him—but nowhere near to my six-two.

Persistent, I gave him that.

But only one man burrowed beneath my skin, and I couldn't seem to rid my mind of him.

———

I arrived at Clyde's Cafe before Jacob did and chose a seat against the far wall where I could watch the door. I'd done a bit of indulging since getting back to Philly and had enjoyed every second of living it up. Seeing as how I'd had another killer workout, I ordered myself a frou-frou coffee with caramel sauce and extra whipped cream.

Iced, of course.

A decadent dessert, sweet enough to give me a goddamn buzz without a lick of liquor.

Jacob arrived a few minutes after I did, waved, and waited in line to order a drink. At three-thirty in the afternoon, he wore a suit and tie, so I expected he'd come straight from the day school.

He still moved and smiled the same, but he wasn't the mischievous kid I'd known. A few inches taller, he'd gotten a good twenty pounds heavier, looking more like his dad Rick than his tiny mom and little brother.

"Sorry to keep you waiting," he said, sliding into the chair across from me and holding a to-go cup with a sleeve around it.

"You aren't late." I grinned and clasped his hand atop the table. "It's good to finally see you, Jacob."

"Yeah—life." He shrugged and sipped his coffee. "The kids are practicing for their end of the year celebration at the day school, and between that, soccer, and piano lessons, there isn't much time to breathe."

Yep. Hearing about the accomplishments I had yet to make twisted my stomach right back up.

"Is Trish still a stay-at-home mom now that the kids are in school full time?"

"Yeah." Jacob settled more into his chair, tugging

his tie loose. "We'd agreed she would go back to work once the kids were older, but I like having her at home. There's a level of comfort in knowing she's there if the kids need anything."

And him too, I imagined, the lucky fucker.

"I'm glad you two get along so well," I said. "Sorry I missed the wedding."

I'd been overseas at the time on a business trip, one I hadn't been able to reschedule or cancel last minute like their wedding had been. We'd both been bummed I couldn't stand beside him, but when you decide you've found the love of your life and get hitched less than a month later, you can't have all your wishes fulfilled.

"You were there in spirit."

I nodded and sipped down some sweetness, thinking about how we'd lost touch after that summer. But I didn't blame Trish. I'd been enamored with Shannon in the beginning, allowing everything and everyone else in my life to take a back seat too.

But his marriage and happiness lasted while mine had shit the bed.

"So, what's your plan now that you're back?" Jacob asked, and I shrugged, glancing around the cafe, feeling aimless as fuck.

Murmurs rose from those around us along with the noisier sounds of the various coffee machines, but the joint smelled like comfort—coffee and muffins.

"I'm doing some odd design side jobs, but I sold my business and don't have to rush into something else right now. Kinda letting everything settle in my head. Process. That sort of shit."

Jacob nodded, his steady stare on my face. "Trish and I have been praying for you, for God's guidance."

While I appreciated the sentiment, I couldn't care less about Jacob's God or whatever path they thought he might have for me.

I made my own way in life. Of course, I hadn't chosen right every time, but that was what a man in love oftentimes did.

"Thanks," I stated the right thing rather than telling Jacob not to bother.

"I've been meaning to invite you over to Mom's for Sunday dinner."

A grin broke over my face. "Like old times at Sherry and Rick's dining room table?"

"Without all the ruckus, yeah. My twins are much more behaved than we ever were."

"Remember when your mom made those sweet and sour green beans?"

Jacob's face stretched into a grimace. "Ugh. You had to bring that one up."

"How about when she used salt instead of sugar in the strawberry pie?"

He barked out a laugh, and we spent the next half-hour reminiscing about what used to be.

Eventually, we sobered, and he took on that studying focus again.

"How are you doing, Aiden? I know we've grown apart over the years, and the few times we talked on the phone, you seemed...different. How is your walk with the Lord?"

"There is no walk." My blunt, honest answer caused the corners of his eyes to downturn like my words disappointed him. I expected they did. His world revolved around God and the church.

But he'd asked, and I wasn't about to sugarcoat what I knew would hurt his heart.

"I'm praying now that you're home, you'll find His path for your life again."

Don't count on it.

"He has your best interest in heart, Aiden," Jacob continued when I didn't offer a comment and sucked down some room temp frou-frou coffee. "He wants all of His children to live holy lives, ones pleasing to him."

And what about the things *we* wanted, I was tempted to ask. But again, I kept my mouth shut and gave my focus to the final swigs of sweetness in my cup.

Jed might have the title of pastor, but his older brother embodied the word to the point of becoming pushy. Thank fuck Jed was more laid back and private about his spirituality. Hanging with him and watching movies had become the highlight of my existence.

"I know you're struggling right now." Jacob laid his hand over my wrist and squeezed. "But I'm trusting God for you. Just know I'm here if you need anything."

"I appreciate it," I said with a fake-as-fuck smile, my insides more unsettled than they'd been in years.

Jacob and I had more than drifted apart as friends. We'd gone in direct opposition to one another after I'd left Philly. The solid friendship had dissolved to the point I itched to get up and take off.

I finished my drink and shifted, readying to do just that.

"So—Sunday dinner at least?"

Fuck.

"Sure," I agreed anyway, but not because of wanting to spend time with him and his family that would, without doubt, make me even more jealous over what he'd attained.

It would be good to see Rick and Shelly who'd never treated me as anything but a third son.

And I had no qualms over spending a couple of extra hours with his little brother.

9

JED

I sat at my desk, daydreaming about my and Aiden's movie marathon the previous couple of nights. Takeout, the final three Star Wars films, and the fluffy socks Aiden continued to tease me about.

My toes were always cold—winter, spring, or summer—it seemed I couldn't make them warm no matter what I did. Luckily I'd never married and didn't have a wife to bitch over my freezing feet against her warm legs while cuddling in bed.

I wondered how Aiden would react to my frozen toes in that situation.

A heavy exhale sank me further into my chair as I attempted to ignore the sudden butterflies in my stomach. Staring out my office window, I wondered what he was up to. He'd met with Jacob the day before over at Clyde's Cafe, their first get-together since he'd returned home.

Jacob hadn't invited him over to his and Trish's place for dinner, hadn't made time for his old friend who'd been nothing but faithful to him.

I knew my brother was busy, but had I been in his shoes, I'd have changed my entire schedule the day Aiden arrived.

The Aiden I'd come to know was different than the kid Jacob had spent twenty-four-seven with, and I couldn't imagine their lives would mesh like they used to though.

Aiden hadn't offered any details about their coffee date beyond a "good," and I didn't poke for more since that wasn't my way.

He had told me the night before how he had sold his business to completely start over in Philly, and he toyed with some new ideas beyond the bit of side work he did designing flyers for a local company. It seemed he floated aimlessly in his existence, but I hadn't offered counsel like I was sure Jacob had done.

Always the shepherd, Jacob made other people's business his own to help guide them through life. God knew I'd felt his verbal prods plenty the previous sixteen years.

But Aiden had no interest in God or the church, that much I'd easily guessed at considering the things he'd said in all our hours together. Surprisingly, he didn't push to get more information from me or suggest a different walk after all I had admitted to. He didn't judge, and even though he spun my mind, I found a sense of comfort in him I hadn't with anyone else—family included.

But no matter my level of ease, he still woke sinful urges inside me that I was powerless to suppress. At least I had the willpower to keep from crawling over the couch and straddling his powerful thighs. Tasting his mouth. Biting his neck and leaving suck marks over his skin.

Damnit, the man made me feel like a teenager again after years of a quiet libido. I loved it. Hated it.

A knock sounded on my door, and I let out a heavy exhale, bringing my brain back online with all things church and work. Renee had already asked me about retrieving something from the church's cafe when she'd left for lunch a few minutes earlier.

Pastor Welker would have waltzed right into my office without announcing his arrival.

"Come on in!" I called out to whoever wished to visit or gossip, hoping for the first.

Jamie, one of the young men who worked with the church's treasurer, Mr. Bowers, entered, a manila envelope in hand. He glanced over his thin shoulder into the reception area before shutting the door.

I wondered if Mr. Bowers had been talking about Renee's husband—and also wondered what kind of earful of bull I was about to hear considering his shifty glance and unusually quiet feet.

Face a bit pale, Jamie attempted a smile that

didn't reach his eyes like it normally would have. The kid seemed perpetually happy.

"Have a seat," I offered, my senses on alert.

He did as told, his butt perched on the edge of the chair. "There's a...well." Jamie inhaled deeply and let it out with a rush. "I-I think I've found something." He slammed his eyelids shut as his voice wavered. "I *know* I found something."

Definitely not Renee and her husband's sex life.

"Jamie?" I pushed when he didn't expound, and the silence grew enough that unease slid through my mind and tingled my spine.

"Here." He hopped to his feet and spread out the papers from the envelope, pointing at the first, a printed-off spreadsheet. "I've highlighted in yellow the treasurer's report for last month, and here in orange"—he centered beneath me another paper with cramped penciled numbers—"you'll see they don't match up. And these deposit slip copies...well, I'm pretty sure..." Jamie's voice trailed off, and he sank back into his chair as though out of steam and exhausted.

I did see. Clearly.

A massive discrepancy appeared against the numbers written by hand after offerings had been collected and the totals entered into the treasurer's report and on the photocopied images of deposit slips.

"Who counts the offering, Jamie?" I asked,

keeping my voice low while checking the tallies for the month before the one he had pointed out.

"I do, sir." His voice barely rose above a whisper.

Shit.

"And how many times before handing things over to Mr. Bowers?"

"Three." Jamie swallowed and rubbed his palms down his slacks. "And he double-counts in front of me before readying the deposits in his own office."

I couldn't tear my focus off the damning evidence. "Does he take the deposits to the bank?"

"Pastor Welker does every Monday morning at ten like clockwork."

Double shit.

I pulled out my calculator, praying Jamie had added wrong. Every single week of the previous three months proved he hadn't. The deposits didn't reflect what the church had taken in—by close to twelve thousand dollars.

My mouth dried out, and adrenaline leaked into my bloodstream, causing my hands to shake. "Is Mr. Bowers aware you've made copies of these deposit slips?"

"No—I, uh...well, after I came across the spreadsheet—by accident, I swear—I got to thinking. Puzzles are my thing, you know?"

I didn't.

"And I had to get to the bottom of this." Jamie shifted on his chair, studying his hands clasped on his lap beneath his stooped shoulders. "I saw where Mr. Bowers keeps the safe key," he whispered.

"It's okay, Jamie," I said, trying for a smile and calm tone even though I felt anything but. "You did right by bringing this to me. You're not going to get into trouble for seeking out the truth."

A pile of steaming *shit* truth that didn't bode well for Simply Grace Church.

Pastor Welker.

Myself.

Being in a position of authority, it would be my responsibility to hold people accountable for their actions—even though I had secret ones of my own.

But sinful lusts in my head and body didn't affect anyone but me. Stealing from the church, from a flock of people who admired and looked to you for spiritual leadership was another story, one that burned inside my guts.

My parents would be devastated, and a church upheaval could affect Jacob's job as the day school's principal.

Biting back curses, I piled the papers together. "I'm going to make copies of these, Jamie—but not here at the church. Is it okay for me to hold onto this for the time being?"

"You're the only man I trust at the moment because you don't ever gossip, and you aren't nosey... but what should I do?"

"Keep vigilant, and don't stir anything up outside

the two of us, okay? Let's take our time, evaluate the evidence, and pray long and hard before deciding on a course of action. Obviously, something is afloat here, but we can't just go spewing what I'm hoping turns up to be nothing more than a mistake."

As if.

Jamie let out a heavy exhale and nodded. "You're one of the few genuine and honest people in this administration, Pastor Jed."

My throat tightened. I was anything but genuine —or honest. Too many masks hid my truth from the world as was necessary in the life I'd chosen.

But I thanked Jamie for his kind words before sending him on his way.

Stuffing the envelope into my briefcase, I offered up a prayer for strength, for wisdom, expecting even while doing so that I wouldn't get a single word in reply.

I called Dad on speakerphone on my way home, needing that sense of grounding I always felt from talking to him. We chatted for a few minutes about the usual—sports and fishing, eventually settling my insides enough I could breathe evenly.

"Do you ever wish you'd chosen a different profession?" My question came out of left field, but I decided to ride the wave.

"Everything okay, son?" Dad asked rather than answering.

Since I stopped at a red light, I closed my eyes for

a few seconds. How was it parents were so damn discerning even when on the phone?

"I just had a long day, and I'm overwhelmed."

"If you're wondering about your choice to go into the ministry," Dad stated quietly, "only you can answer that one, Jed. You have the heart for it, no question. I've heard countless times from other church members that your empathy during their sickness or grief brings them comfort."

I couldn't shepherd like Jacob, but I had strengths of my own, ones God could use.

"I'm on the right path, then," I murmured, taking some of Dad's assurance as my own.

"We have to trust God in all things—even the daily nine-to-five part of living on this earth."

That meant giving the Welker and church money issue to God.

Once off the phone, I did just that, hoping that for once—just once—the Holy Spirit would guide my steps on how to handle the mess Jamie had unearthed.

10

———

AIDEN

Five full days back home and I needed to find something other than the gym and hanging with Jed to occupy my mind. A new business venture, a part-time job at the least until I decided what I wanted to do.

Creating cartoons in my spare hours thanks to Jed's reminders and prompting eased tension in my shoulders and made me smile, but my hand ached.

And my feet drew me outside my apartment to Jed's door—even while knowing he wasn't home.

Creep.

I ignored the word in my head and let myself into his quiet, dark apartment. He kept the blinds shut while he spent the day at work as though trying to shut out the world from learning who he was on the inside.

A private man who intrigued the hell out of me

and visited my dreams even though I thought I was straight.

Or maybe I was more angled, bent a bit, than I'd assumed. Jed certainly twisted me up, and my need to know more, dig deep inside his brain to learn his thoughts, spurred me on.

I'd feared an addiction while at the lowest point in my existence, but instead of vodka or whiskey like I'd expected, *all things Jed* had proven to be what I craved.

He lingered in my head while I penciled characters to life, and I imagined his face lighting up while telling me their stories. Outlandish, laughable, same as his tales had been as a teenager.

He'd loved spinning words together, had told the best ghost stories that Jacob and I hadn't given him shit for. His childlike wonder had always made me grin.

And the adult version of Padawan, his serious side, needed straightening out in my head since I couldn't align the two persons in the reality of our "now."

I stood in his bedroom doorway before I thought my actions through.

His laptop sat open on his desk, the screen dark.

My pulse picked up, a sense of doing wrong tingling the back of my mind, but I ignored the feeling, a simple touch to the mouse bringing Jed's laptop to life.

No request for a fingerprint, no password request.

Why would he? Jed never invited people into his space—but he'd allowed the worst wolf of them all to weasel in. A damn bloodhound who couldn't let anything lie, just like Shannon had always accused me of.

I opened his browser and accessed his history—and his secrets unfolded with a few clicks of the mouse.

A treasure trove better than his bedstand.

I sank into his chair and rolled close, the screen before my wide eyes holding me captive. The man had bookmarked countless websites, but I started at the top. While his toys had suggested he would take and give dick without complaint, I'd expected he tended toward being a bottom considering his size and all.

But the aggressive, bossy twink topping a bear in his favorite porn video?

Curiosity could easily kill the cat lurking in my head.

A beefy guy bottoming, his deep voice egging his lover on to fuck him deeper, harder...

My dick swelled, leaking the longer I watched.

Couldn't. Look. Away.

Who knew gay porn could be so damn hot? The twink had a long, thin dick, and he stabbed away at the hairy ass in front of him, his whimpers and gasps higher pitched and strained. Hotter than the noises escaping the one he called his bear.

"That's it, wildcat," the bigger guy coaxed his twink on. "Give it to me—give me that pretty cock, boy. Yeah. Yeah, wildcat, just like that..."

"Fucking hell." I groaned and grabbed hold of my balls to calm the fuck down as both men onscreen ramped up their vocal appreciation of each other, their climaxes drawing close.

The twink shattered first, shaking and quaking while filling the bigger guy's ass with cum. He pulled out, breaths hard as the camera zoomed in to capture the ooze of white from a puckered hole.

"Shove it back in, baby," the deep voice demanded, and a slender finger gathered up cum and pressed into the asshole front and center on the computer screen. "Mmm. Fucking love when you breed me, wildcat."

Shit.

I clicked out of the browser, my heart racing and my dick like granite. Creep didn't begin to describe how I felt at that moment. It was like I'd peeled back Jed's scalp and burrowed into his brain.

One simple porn video had told me more than he would ever admit to.

And what I'd learned only made my obsession that much more intense. There was no longer any point in denying that the thought of Jed becoming a voracious kitty for dick turned me the fuck *on.*

In my mind, it was Jed violating my body with *his* pretty little dick when I stroked myself off in the shower five minutes later. I'd never been interested in ass play even though Shannon had suggested it, but the thought of Jed touching me there? Taking his pleasure, shuddering, and breeding me?

I came so damn hard stars exploded behind my eyelids and I went weak in the knees.

I, Aiden McNellis, once upon a time lover of women and all things pussy and tits, craved dick.

Jed's to be precise.

Mom hadn't been too far off the mark.

And I was just asshole enough to want to corrupt him—and set him free to live a life outside the prison he'd put himself in.

———

Me: **Would you do me a HUGE favor?**

I waited, staring at my cell screen while waiting for Jed to reply, but I knew he wouldn't let me down. It wasn't like the poor guy had anything else to take up his time.

Wildcat: **Sure.**

Smirking over the new nickname I'd assigned him in my cell, I typed out what I drooled for. **Cheesesteak from Sully's, pretty please? I'm starved for some juicy meat and cheesy sauce.**

A snort of laughter left me as I imagined what

the text would do to Jed's imagination. He had a hell of a good one.

Wildcat took a bit of time before typing back, but I expected he squeaked the repeated word, **Sure.**

Me: **Can't wait.** I added a wink emoji for shits and giggles, but I expected he let out a groan instead.

Jed's coming and going was like clockwork, so ten minutes before his usual arrival time—allotted for stopping at Sully's—I pulled off my shirt and did a few push-ups even though I'd worn my ass out at the gym earlier that morning.

Michael, after I'd convinced him I wasn't interested in dick, had suggested we workout together since we'd showed up within minutes of each other every morning that week.

A cool guy, a few months off drugs and booze and settling into the sober life—he made an excellent lifting buddy our first day spotting one another even though he'd given me all sorts of shit.

The dude was harmless, just a major horn dog who teased and didn't follow through from what I'd seen.

I might not swing the dick way like Michael, but I definitely leaned toward Jed's. Just the thought of him watching his favorite porn video, lips parted and cheeks pink while jerking off...yeah.

I wanted in on that shit.

That indulgent trait in the back of my mind that

had come into play after leaving California had found a new focus, and fuck if I had any desire to ignore it.

His knock came while I still hugged the floor, and I hopped up, my pulse thrumming from more than the fifty push-ups I'd done. Butterflies, of all fucking things, bothered my gut as I reached for the door.

And they exploded at Jed's expression when he came face to chest with my bare skin.

"Shit," he whispered and gulped, shoving a paper bag at me.

Rather than plucking my dinner from his hand, I grasped his wrist to keep him from spinning away from me. A glance down gave me an eyeful of tenting dress pants before he yanked his briefcase in front of his groin.

Grinning at him, I *did* snag the bag from his hand. "Thanks, Jed."

He dipped his head in a quick nod and hurried across the hallway.

God, that ass. "Any plans tonight?"

His hand shook while he tried to unlock his door.

"I created a new cartoon character today," I said as he finally sank the key into the lock. "I'd love to show it to you."

Excuses to get the wildcat into my lair but at least I didn't lie.

"Um...okay, yeah. Just...I need to shower. Eat. And stuff."

Stuff.

I bit back my grin. "Come whenever you want."

I swore he muttered another curse before shutting his door between us. Chuckling, I adjusted my dick and went into my kitchen to devour my dinner.

It took Jed over two hours to find the balls to take me up on my offer. I honestly didn't expect him to show. I'd waited for my cell to ding with an excuse to avoid the big bad wolf.

I answered the door to find his face more pale than pink, his shoulders slouched. As usual, he wouldn't look at me or my chest I'd kept bare just for his viewing pleasure.

Stroke my ego.

"Thought you were going to bail on our date," I joked as he shuffled past me into my apartment.

He shrugged, and I realized it was more than timidity closing him off from me.

"You okay?" I asked, steering him toward my couch.

Jed slumped down, his head tipped back, arms hanging at his sides. He appeared wasted emotionally when usually he was a bottled-up soda ready to explode around me. "Just some shit from work."

A third curse in one day. What was the world coming to?

Rather than tease or poke, I sat beside him, angling to study his face.

Definitely pale—almost haggard. His lips pressed into a tight line, a furrow deep in his brow.

I squeezed his shoulder without thought, and a shudder rippled over him. He swallowed hard but didn't pull away from my hold.

"Hey...what's going on, Jed?"

"I-I can't talk about it, but thanks for your offer of an ear." Jed lifted his head and tried for a smile that didn't reach his eyes.

I kept my grip on his shoulder. "Need a hug?"

Heat flared, and he jerked his focus off my chest for the hands clenched together on his lap. "I-I'm good."

"It's Friday night," I said, letting go of his shoulder and getting up to head into the kitchen. "Want to just lose ourselves in some good sci-fi and forget about the world for a while?"

"Sounds like heaven," Jed muttered from behind me.

I could show him an even better heaven—

Lousy lay.

Fucking hell, Shannon's words bounced around in my brain, sending my thoughts straight toward shit. How had I put up with her for so damn long? Why did I even let her negativity affect me as it did? I'd never had one complaint about my skills in bed before her.

As much as I would like to think the issue had been hers, she'd managed to make her digs stick. Like goddamn Superglue.

Grabbing a couple of beers, I shook my head. I slammed the fridge door a little too hard before striding back to the living room area.

"Here." I tossed the beer at Jed, and he had no choice but to catch it.

"I don't drink."

"Tonight, you do," I told him with my best Yoda voice while flopping back on the couch. "At least crack the fucking thing so we can toast to the shit that's our lives."

I could feel Jed's gaze on me, but I pulled one of his habits—I didn't look at him.

With the clicker in hand, I navigated to Disney+ which I'd subscribed to on a whim earlier that day. *A New Hope's* theme song burst to life, words sliding away on an angle across the screen.

I tossed the clicker aside, opened my beer, and finally gave Jed my full attention. "I figured we could start at the real beginning—or we can watch something else? I heard *Firefly* was pretty good."

"It is—but this is fine." He peered at me, his brow slightly furrowed, but I knew he wouldn't dig into my head about my odd subscription thing. "Okay," he muttered to himself. A crack and fizz, and Jed lifted his beer. "Cheers?"

I nodded and clinked my can to his.

"I'm sorry you had a shit day," he said while I swallowed down half my drink in one long guzzle.

"I didn't. Just a moment. Sorry about yours."

Jed turned his focus on the flatscreen I'd hung on the wall. He took a tentative sip of beer, grimacing.

"Well?" I asked.

"Bad." Another grimace twisted his face. "The taste of this shit might just be worse than the day job."

Day job—not a calling, not a passion.

A definite prison, one that caused more curses to spill out of his lips in the previous fifteen minutes than I'd heard in his entire life.

Jacob definitely should have chosen the route their grandfathers had insisted on instead of his little brother who wasn't cut from the same cloth.

"Give me that," I ordered, gesturing toward Jed's can, that part of me wanting to help set Jed free becoming more than just a temptation.

He handed over his beer without complaint, our fingers brushing.

And there went the pink flush spreading over his face.

I grinned, settled in with two beers in my hands, and lost myself in Jed's favorite movie.

Biding my time until he was ready to see the light.

11

———

JED

Family dinner that week after church didn't appeal to me.

At all.

Pastor Welker had preached about honesty and integrity—in the workplace and at home, not just as a face for other believers. His hypocrisy knew no bounds—and I hated being associated with him.

My stomach churned while he spoke, and my desire to sink into the floor and disappear where I sat behind him on stage ended up being more real than I'd ever experienced.

Even prior to the sermon while I took the pulpit to give the announcements and pray over our service, I'd felt out of sorts. Out of place. Wrong in the skin God had given me.

Walking into my parents' home after service for a family meal only worsened my unease.

Aiden stood with Jacob across the living room.

Our gazes clashed, and I quickly looked away, not having to force my grin as my niece and nephew threw themselves at my legs as though they were still toddlers thinking they could topple Uncle Jed over.

I was the short tree, they'd always said, their dad the tall one who couldn't be budged.

A stoic oak, I agreed in my head. Unmoved in his faith, his life built upon the same foundation as mine—but his flourished, offering fulfillment I would never know.

Jealousy twinged through me as I watched him and Aiden in my periphery. Standing close, chatting quietly as though no time had passed. Aiden had been Jacob's friend first, and I would protect my heart by remembering that fact.

"Jed." Dad's gruff greeting pulled my focus from the blondes hugging my legs for the recliner he always sat in. His smile didn't match up with his tone, but that was just Dad.

"How are you?" I asked, peeling the twin seven-year-olds off me. They scampered into the kitchen where Trish probably helped Mom finish getting dinner ready.

"Good," Dad said, studying my face. "You?"

I nodded, knowing he checked in with me after that phone conversation earlier in the week.

"Well done with the announcements this morning," he offered when I didn't give a verbal reply.

I squeezed Dad's shoulder, his weekly words of edification soaking into my skin and easing my negativity over Jacob's accomplishments. Petty, but I took pride in having their praise for standing at a pulpit when my older brother only occupied the day school's principal's desk.

"Are you still volunteering over at the nursing home on Tuesdays?" he asked, his focus turning back toward the TV.

"Yeah. It's the highlight of my week, actually." I'd sat with Mr. Williams the entire hour when I should have also visited the woman across the hallway, but something about the man drew me. I longed to hear more about his life, to relish in the truth that sometimes gay men could have a happily ever after.

"Dinner is ready!" Mom called from the kitchen. "Let's eat before the roast dries out!"

We all shuffled into the dining room, Jacob's kids noisy as usual until their butts hit the chairs. Like they donned angel robes and halos, they quieted down, hands on their laps.

Mr. Williams had lost three younger siblings and an infant nephew for choosing Jonathan, and just the thought of the same happening to me swelled my throat.

But the twins' flashing smiles revealed the inner devilry I couldn't get enough of, and it proved contagious.

The three of us shared winks that weren't as secret as I pretended.

Mom caught my gaze and smiled, and Trish, on my other side, patted my arm with sisterly affection I soaked up.

"Good to see you, Jed," she murmured.

Silence settled, and I glanced around the table at everyone except Aiden—who sat to my left. Hands lifted and clasped with those beside them like every Sunday for Dad's blessing over the food.

Aiden's warm palm slid along mine, and it took all my willpower to keep from squeaking, moaning, and melting.

Thank God for Mom's tablecloth that fell onto our laps and hid what his touch did to my groin or Trish would have gotten an eyeful.

He clasped my hand with firm fingers, and I bowed my head, not hearing a damn word from Dad's mouth. Warmth swept up through my arm, down through my body, and I knew my face had to be red. Parting my lips, I struggled to steady my breath and heartbeat, needing calm before the Amen that would open the eyes around the table.

Please, God, help me.

Nothing. My dick stayed hard, my face hot.

Amens echoed around the table, but for once, I didn't agree. Keeping my head down, I fumbled with my napkin, willing away the strain against my slacks.

Aiden elbowed me, and I closed my eyes briefly

—then I realized he held out the bowl of potatoes. Grasping at something else to keep my hands and thoughts occupied, I took it from him, surprised my fingers didn't shake as my insides did.

"Aiden said he's living across the hall from you," Mom said, forcing me to give someone other than myself attention.

"He is."

"Why didn't you mention it when we spoke on the phone the other day?"

I'd called her the day after I'd talked to Dad, needing another dose of assurance. Like him, she'd told me to trust God.

I shrugged, accepting the green beans from Aiden and glancing across the table at my brother to take the focus off me. "I can't believe you didn't tell us he was coming back home."

Aiden bumped his knee against mine with firm intent, but I ignored him—or tried to, rather.

Jacob glanced between me and his friend where he sat flanked by the twins who knew better than to misbehave with their father close by. "I've been kind of busy at work."

Same excuse as always when it came to my brother not having time to speak to me.

"I realized I hadn't told you," Jacob continued, "but Aiden had already informed me the two of you had met in the hallway his first day back."

"What are the chances," Mom said, her voice

bright as always. "It's like our third son has returned to us."

Son.

That singular word reminded me all over again of why my fantasy of loving who my heart wanted would never come to fruition. Not that I would ever find the gall to leave the only life I could fathom.

If Mom knew the man Aiden had become, I wondered if she would continue to consider him as such. He wasn't the good kid she remembered who'd faithfully attended church with us every Sunday and Wednesday night for youth group.

Aiden might still have perfect manners and know what to say around those who expected good behavior, but I'd seen inside his head enough to figure out his true heart.

"You have to sit with us next Sunday, Aiden," Mom went on. "I can't believe we didn't run into you this morning during service."

He'd told me he wouldn't set foot in a church ever again on Friday when I brought up the suggestion my parents would love to see him. After finding more evidence of Welker's dishonesty over the week, I'd begun to feel the same.

But I didn't have a choice.

Curling up on a couch with him on Sunday mornings to binge *Firefly* would have been ten times more enjoyable.

"I couldn't make it, Shelly," Aiden lied smoothly.

"Well, next week, I insist you sit with us. It's such a pleasure seeing Jedediah on stage behind Pastor Welker. He's such a good man." Mom went on to gush, pushing Dad on occasion to add his grunts of agreement while I sat silent about the liar who led the flock at Simply Grace Church.

Aiden's knee brushed against mine again—and held still.

I fought to swallow the dry roast even though I'd covered it in gravy.

"Aiden tells me you've been hanging out quite a bit," Jacob said, causing me to choke on my food. A bite of annoyance laced his words, and I wondered if Mom taking pride in my life choices irked him in that moment or the fact I'd got to spend more time with Aiden than he did.

"Oh, that's lovely!" Mom said before I responded.

"He's showed me all the Star Wars movies I've missed out on," Aiden said, a smile in his voice while heat once more licked at my face.

"Pizza, cheesesteaks…" Jacob's snippy tone lifted my head. He glanced between us again. "I'm feeling a little left out."

"I offered," Aiden said with light laughter that sounded forced to my ears, "but you've been too busy."

Thank goodness.

"Jacob." Trish, his wife elbowed him. "You ought to take an evening for yourself this week and hang out with Aiden." I wondered if she just wanted a few nighttime hours to herself. God knew if I'd been married to a grump like Jacob, I would have.

"Maybe I will." Jacob went back to his meal but glanced up at me quickly, his brow furrowed.

For the first time ever, I grew uncomfortable by my brother's attention.

Jealousy all around, I supposed, but that didn't ease the sad ping in my chest.

The chatter around the table turned toward the grandkids, how first grade was going for them at the day school and all the things grandmothers loved hearing about while I allowed myself to partake in whatever it was going on beneath the table.

Aiden's knee stayed put.

So did mine.

Immediately after dinner, Aiden claimed he had some business calls to take care of and made his escape before I got a chance to talk to him. Dad sat in his recliner, and the kids were in the kitchen with Mom and Trish.

I'd grabbed my keys off the hallway table, ready to say my goodbyes, but Jacob cornered me by the front door.

"I see your crush hasn't waned."

Shit.

My heart seized at his quiet suggestion, and I fought the need to pluck at my collar and tie suddenly choking me.

"I never told Mom and Dad," he continued when I couldn't force my voice to deny what he'd claimed.

"What makes you think I...uh..." I struggled to find words.

He huffed a sarcastic snort of laughter. "Please, Jed. You were so damn obvious. I can't believe they didn't figure it out back then too."

He'd kept his mouth shut, kept my secret to himself—kept me from being a disappointment to our grandfathers.

Thankfulness flooded through my soul, and the annoyance I'd felt for him earlier fell away, allowing me to breathe again. My big brother had protected me when he had every right in the eyes of God to uncover my sinful nature.

"I thought you gave that part of you up for God when you chose the ministry."

"I did," I whispered a partial truth of what he'd known and had kept quiet about.

Jacob would never understand it wasn't possible to just set aside a portion of yourself that helped make up the whole.

"Don't give in to temptation, Jed." His tone sounded firm like Dad's had when we'd been kids and got into trouble. "And don't mess with Aiden. He has troubles enough, and I won't stand for you corrupting his soul."

I stared at my shined black shoes, once more upset with him and unable to find the words to express the rioting mess in my guts. He assumed I would lead Aiden down a dark path, but as my brother, shouldn't he have feared the other way around?

"He finally escaped that devil of a woman, and I'm going to do everything I can to encourage him to find his strength where he did as a kid—in God."

Jacob obviously had no clue of the man Aiden had become, how his morals had changed.

Lifting my head, I eyed my brother. He wasn't a violent homophobe, but he called homosexuality a sin. Unnatural perversion due to the fall of mankind.

"I've chosen my life, Jacob," I reminded him when I didn't have to. "And I have no wish to corrupt your friend—*my* friend—either. But if hanging out with him to watch movies you think are stupid and worldly help ease whatever trouble he's going through, then I'll gladly be there for him. Maybe you should consider being an ear, a shoulder, rather than trying to shepherd him toward God."

Jacob blinked down at me, and I realized I had never once stood up to him or suggested he live a different way than his usual controlling one.

"I'll see you later." I walked out of Mom and Dad's without saying goodbye to either of them, Trish, or the kids, but I'd needed to escape before Jacob lit into me with all his grumpy dogmatism I wasn't in the mood for.

Bad enough I had the shit of the church rattling

around into my brain like a one-man band, but everything I had chosen in life was called into question because of one person.

I wondered what trouble Aiden had faced, the reasons for his return home. Shannon hadn't come up in too many of our conversations, and I wouldn't ever push for information. Perhaps I needed to change my means of communication. Maybe talking about Aiden's pain would help him. He seemed comfortable with me—perhaps a bit too much than was appropriate, but I'd taken solace in his touch beneath the table.

Arousing, but also comforting.

Something that would definitely intensify my addiction to him if given the opportunity.

My mind a jumble of riotous thoughts, I headed home and breathed a sigh of relief—yet didn't like—that Aiden didn't text to invite me over.

I'm glad he didn't, I thought while punching my pillow beneath my head a few hours later when I attempted to sleep.

But I lied to myself, something I'd become quite good at doing with everyone around me—especially my family.

Guilt should have pulled me from my bed and onto my knees for a time of prayer, but I rolled over and lost myself in dreams of wide shoulders and twinkling hazel eyes instead.

12

———

AIDEN

I swore Jed avoided me all damn week long, and I took my annoyance out at the gym every morning.

By Friday, he'd brushed off my texted invites to hang out four times, and I wondered if I'd gone too far with the whole knee under the table thing. It wasn't like he'd pulled away from my touch though.

"What crawled up your hole and croaked?" Michael asked as we stood side by side doing sets of overhead dumbbell presses.

"My love life sucks ass."

"I hear that—but sucking ass is a good thing. You ought to consider dick instead of pussy. Easier to get without all the mess."

"Shut the fuck up."

Michael chuckled while I frowned. "Sway our way," he insisted with his teasing tone, same as he did at least once a morning while we worked out together. "You'd be surprised by how easy it is to get along with a male lover than a female. Emotions don't tangle into the equation, and there's no guessing what's going on inside the other's head."

"It's just busting a nut in a willing hole," I repeated what he'd told me a few days prior. "I understand, really."

Michael laughed, but I caught the hesitancy in his eyes in the wall of mirrors we faced.

We both set down the dumbbells and took a breather, and I watched him as his hungry gaze roamed over the gym's occupants.

"When's the last time you got laid?" I asked, poking as I always did.

"Eight months and five days ago."

My eyebrows popped up. The man had me beat —but I never would've thought that possible considering how much he enjoyed discussing dicks. "Is Grindr failing you or have you lost your mojo?"

A small smile lifted the corner of his mouth as he turned his focus to the floor in the first act of shyness I'd seen the man portray. "Neither. I...uh, gave up sex when I decided to get clean. They went hand in hand for me, you know?"

"I don't."

"Keeping my dick to myself helps me stay sober," he tried to explain.

"Like a cigarette and booze for some?"

"Kinda, yeah. Like peanut butter and jelly too." Michael glanced around the gym again, all trace of his usual cocky confidence taking a back seat to insecurity that made him more approachable. And likable, even though I felt he was pretty cool for a cocky asshole. "I hit rock bottom and knew I needed to turn my life around before I ended up six feet under sixty years too soon."

"Good choice."

He nodded and picked back up his dumbbells. "Sometimes a simple change, a yes rather than a no, can alter the course of your life and create something ten times more rewarding—even if it means taking a break from dick and entering detox."

I grabbed my dumbbells for our last set, chewing over his words. They ended up sticking with me through the night while I stewed over what to do about my attraction to Jed.

I wanted to get all up in his space, to force a confrontation so he would come out to me once and for all. Then I would kiss him senseless and give him that yes Michael had suggested.

Make a change.

But still, Shannon's words echoed in my brain, shutting me down.

Instead of taking a chance and texting Jed, I settled on my bed and pulled up his favorite porn site. It took all of ten seconds to find the video he had bookmarked.

Watching the wildcat and his bear go at it again worked me up to hard and aching. I searched the real couple's uploads and viewed two more where they switched positions, their hunger for each other evident in every shared word, caress, and selfless loving on one another.

Different from what I'd always known with Shannon, and ten times more powerful.

I ended up with a load of spunk over my torso—and Jed's name on my lips.

———

Needing to see him, I took that damn invite from Shelly and went to Simply Grace on Sunday morning. I dragged ass after having been up into the wee hours of the morning—too damn late thanks to my new addiction and feeding the idea of change Michael had enticed my brain to consider. I got to the church after service had already begun.

I ended up sitting near the back, but I could still see Jed in his suit and tie behind Pastor Welker who ranted about honesty and living a holy life.

I tuned the fucker out and studied the man behind him who shifted more than he sat still. Gaze narrowed, I wished I'd sat closer to the stage so I could figure out what the fuck Jed's problem was that kept him as antsy as a kid caught cheating on an exam.

On a whim, I pulled out my cell and shot off a quick text. **You look good in a suit.**

Jed discreetly reached into his coat pocket and placed his cell atop his Bible on his lap which he angled upward. Anyone watching would see he'd attempted to hide his phone.

His head lifted quickly after reading my text, his gaze roaming around the congregation, but I knew he wouldn't see me with how spotlights shone on him and Welker. He went back to his cell.

Wildcat: **You came?**

Hard—twice, last night, I wanted to reply, but I wasn't that much of a sadist. Or maybe I was.

Grinning, I decided on something even worse. **You've always seemed so pious, but that's not true, is it...wildcat?**

Red fused Jed's face harshly enough I could see from the distance separating us.

He didn't reply but lifted his attention to the back of Walker's head. Frozen like a deer in headlights.

Had I gone too far? Worry shifted my ass on the chair, and I started to type out an apology, but someone entered stage left and went straight to Welker as his sermon came to a close.

The man spoke to him quietly, handing him a note, and left.

Welker studied the paper for a few moments before letting out a heavy exhale intentionally into the mic while putting the folded paper into his suit pocket.

He spread his arms wide as though hugging the air, his smile one of tenderness—and disappointment. "We have fallen short, my friends."

Silence reigned.

"The offering collected this morning isn't enough to cover our weekly bills—"

I tuned the fucker out again as Jed visibly shuddered and glanced offstage. My fingers flew over my screen before I thought my words through. **You okay, wildcat?**

Jed stared at the propped-up Bible on his lap and glanced at Welker again while I mentally begged him to reply.

He did.

Wildcat: **Why did you call me that?**

I decided to cover my ass and not fully out what I'd done. What I'd found by snooping into his private life.

Me: **Because I imagine that's what you'd be in the sack. All quiet, shy, and timid for the rest of the world, but I think once that mask is torn off, you'd let loose. Tell me I'm wrong.**

Wildcat: **I wouldn't know.**

The reminder of his virginal state made for a very inappropriate bodily reaction while sitting in a service while the pastor riled his flock up about finances, tithing, and contributing in the knowledge God would provide their needs.

My fucking skin itched with the *need* to flee the atmosphere, the shouted amens rising around me.

Give until it hurts. Trust God.

I wanted to snort at Welker's words, his pleadings to support the church. But that church also supported Jed, paid his salary.

And he'd spent some of that money on things the church definitely wouldn't approve of.

Feeling angsty as fuck and uncomfortable in the dress shirt and tie I'd put on, I went with the devil inside, wanting to rebel against that damn pulpit and all it stood for.

I chose to poke.

Me: **If those toys in your bedstand drawer are any indication, I'd say you'd be a voracious little kitty for the right man.**

Too far, I realized, my grin fading as Jed's face went white—and he stumbled across the back of the stage and disappeared.

I hopped up and rushed out of the sanctuary, hurrying around the side hallway. Sure enough, I caught his backside as he slipped into the men's room at the far end.

Fucking idiot. Lips firmed and all but running, I strode his way, hoping I hadn't completely fucked up.

13

JED

I dropped to my knees and vomited up what was left of my breakfast.

Between Welker's bullshit from the pulpit and Aiden's texts that had shifted the world beneath my feet, I wanted to flush myself down the toilet I hugged.

The door opened, and I knew without looking who entered. "How could you?" I gasped out and gagged again.

I expected an apology, but Aiden didn't speak. Shaking my head, I closed my eyes, trying to talk my stomach into calming down.

I'd never felt so violated in my entire life.

Wildcat—how did he know about my favorite gay couple, my secret indulgence I allowed myself once every couple of months?

I gagged again at the thought that Aiden would get onto my computer without asking.

And he'd found my secret stash of toys.

Bile erupted from my mouth, splattering in the toilet. I spat to rid my mouth of the vile taste.

"Those...things are not mine," I said the first words that came to mind beyond the curses that had rung since I'd read his words.

"Come on, kid." Aiden chuckled, and I listened as his feet brought him closer. "You don't have to lie to me—you think I give a shit about what you're up to in your spare time?"

I had no choice but to deny it.

"I-I don't use them anymore. I gave up that part of my life a long time ago." Eyes still clenched shut, I hung my head over the porcelain bowl, wishing Aiden would just go away. "You have to believe me, Aiden, please."

"No, I don't." He handed me a paper towel, and I snatched it from him. "So you fantasize about fucking yourself on some dude's dick then gifting him with yours. What's the big deal?"

Shit. Shit!

Hell, if anyone heard what he said...

My legs shook like mad, but I stood and pushed past him. "I-I have to go home. I'm sick."

"You aren't sick, Jed, you're simply a man who's attracted to other men, and getting found out has your stomach turned inside—"

Aiden continued with whatever sermon he planned to spew, but I slammed the door behind me, cutting his voice off.

I wasn't attracted to other men.

Just him.

Only him.

I somehow managed to drive my car home without landing in a ditch, and once I shut myself into the privacy of my apartment, I broke down.

My secret sins had been found out, exactly as the Bible promised to those who tried to hide their misdeeds. Guilt should have put me on my knees, but embarrassment and the yearning to sink into the ground and disappear from existence ruled my mind.

Insides twisted, I agonized over wanting to hate my crush and being unable to do so. Aiden would never cross a line enough to make me look upon him with scorn.

And attempting any type of violence in lashing out would only end up with me pulling his hair and tasting the mouth I'd been dreaming of for far too long.

The life I'd chosen, the only one I'd known, didn't allow for wakeful fantasies of him though. I knew what I needed to do.

Every single dildo I owned landed in the trash along with the lube and Fleshlight I'd used the night before for the first time in months.

I stared at my sins atop the remnants of breakfast in my trash can, the sight of them burning into my memory. Being gay wasn't a choice as Jacob had claimed, but living by faith was. I'd had it hammered into my brain for years, and even though I longed for more, for something fulfilling in my life, I couldn't break away.

I didn't know how to, same as the abused wife who kept returning to her husband out of familiarity. Hoping for the best, thinking she could change him, make him love her.

The God of my grandfathers, my parents, wouldn't ever love who I was in the flesh, but still, I clung to the only foundation I had.

Decision made, I slammed my trash can shut, closing myself off from that part of my life.

Emotional exhaustion held new meaning. I curled up on my bed, ignoring the notifications dinging on my cell and staring at baby Yoda on my bureau.

Aiden had crossed a line—several—but his actions had brought me to a necessary crossroads. The desire for freedom, the temptation of what I'd always seen as a sin, fought the morals I'd built my entire life upon.

If Aiden had offered me a beer at that moment, I would have held my nose and downed the whole can, looking for numbness. But I couldn't run from the conflict in my soul. I would avoid him, the unholy temptation that he was until I got my shit straightened out in my head.

And part of that shit included the church finance issues.

The reason there wasn't enough in the bank account to pay the bills as Welker ranted about in the pulpit that morning was because I felt sure he and the treasurer had pocketed the cash for their own use.

Greed, one of the deadly sins.

But no less offensive than lust and envy, both of which I dealt with daily.

Need for fleshly knowledge of Aiden.

Envy of the friends in my recent past who had found love with one another—happiness and contentment. With the same sex.

Who was I to point out the splinter in another's eye and ignore the plank in my own?

I reasoned away my own secret sins with the truth they didn't hurt anyone but myself, but again, I'd been taught that sin was sin. Period.

Dealing with my own was necessary before deciding what to do with what Jamie and I believed pointed to thievery by our pastor and Mr. Bowers. No resolution came to mind, and I finally gave in to the desire to read Aiden's texts.

Mom had sent one first after seeing me stagger off the stage.

I called since I knew she would eventually.

"Are you okay, baby boy?"

"Yeah," I lied, pinching the bridge of my nose. "I had scrambled eggs for breakfast, and they aren't liking my stomach.

"I'll whip up some chicken soup this afternoon just in case."

"I'll be fine, Mom," I said, a smile tilting my lips even though I had nothing but her love to be happy about.

"I'll bring it over tomorrow if you aren't feeling better. Text me in the morning."

"I will, thanks. I appreciate you, Mom."

"Love you." She made kissy noises.

I hung up, my temperature rising as I swiped back into my messages to see what Aiden had to say for himself. As expected, he didn't apologize, but he did call himself all sorts of names, owning every single one.

Creep.

Asshole.

Horny bastard whose best friend's little brother got his brain all fucked up—his words, not mine.

"What?" I whispered, gaze flitting down to the next.

You make me think about things I never considered before, and I don't know what to do with the changes in my mind. The things I feel, what I want.

"Shit." I sat up, finally taking off my dress shoes,

and bit on my lip while reading over that one a second time, my heart kicking into high gear.

Yes, I snooped on your computer after seeing that trove of treasures.

Treasures, not kinky, disgusting sex toys…

I saw the video you bookmarked.

My eyes jumped to the next text.

And it's hot as fuck, Jed. That twink pleasing his bear.

Aiden knew the terms. How far had his curiosity gone into the reaches of sin?

The two of them are so in love, and the way they connect is beautiful. I never had that, never even considered it was possible.

My breath left in a rush. Aiden had written me a damn novel by text, sometimes cutting himself short but picking up where he'd left off on the next.

No fucking way that kind of love and sharing is wrong, Jed. I see your friend Aaron and his Ezra at the gym every morning, and I've talked to them about their friends Zeke and Levi up in Boston. I'm telling you, I've never seen that type of dedication.

Maybe I'm just jaded, fucked up because of my ex.

But maybe I'm not.

**Every heart longs to be accepted and loved. You. Me. Even your dickhead of a brother I still

think of as blood even though he's gone all dogmatic as fuck for his God.

Why can't people see that love is better than hate?

Why do you continue to listen to lies and not allow yourself to just *be*, Jed?

Aiden must have run out of steam after that final text. It'd been a solid twenty minutes without dings.

I rolled to my back and clutched my cell to my chest with shaky hands, every beat of my heart thumping in my ears. Somehow, someway, I'd influenced Aiden. The thought, his words, flooded me with elation, hope even though I'd chosen God's path by tossing out my...treasures.

Unholy temptation.

A loud exhale left me heavy on my bed as a battle raged inside my head, tiring every single cell inside me. Not even the turn of the key in my front door budged me from my fatigue.

Only one person had access to my private life, in more ways than one. I swore the tug of war worsened, my heart raced while also feeling split in half. I studied the backs of my eyelids, listening as Aiden quietly made his way to my bedroom door.

He'd seen every part of me, the darkest reaches of my soul, the silly weirdness of my likes in the comforter beneath me and the old poster hanging above my bed. I wondered what he thought of my Yoda stuffy.

The mattress dipped beside me, and still, he didn't speak.

"You violated my trust, Aiden," I stated quietly, calmer than I expected to be with him in my bed.

"I'm not sorry."

I snorted a laugh but kept my eyes closed. "At least you're honest."

"Intrusive and pushy too. I don't know when to shut up or let things go." Pain laced his voice enough that curiosity forced my eyelids open.

He sat on the edge of my bed, elbows resting on his knees and head hanging low. Guilt seemed to ooze off him, but his slouched shoulders suggested something deeper.

"Hey." I laid my palm on his lower back, and he shivered, goosebumps breaking out over his skin even though it was a tad too warm in my bedroom.

A sense of...power rose to life inside me, and I swallowed hard against the sudden need to pull other reactions from him like my favorite wildcat did from his bear. My hand remained where I'd placed it, my gaze on his face as he turned toward me.

No twinkle lit his eye, nothing but vulnerability hovering in his gaze. "I've rooted out all your secrets, but I can't be sorry because doing so made me realize I can trust you with mine. And I...need that."

He inhaled a shuddered breath and held it.

"Are you okay?" I whispered, wishing I could

hold him rather than offer a simple touch of comfort.

"She fucked me up, Jed." He shook his head and took to glancing around my room. "Fucking toxic words, accusations, gaslighting...I married a psychotic cunt whose purpose in life was to make my last couple months in California a living hell."

A shudder rippled through him, and I couldn't help myself. I crawled over to where he sat and snuggled my chest along his back, my cheek on his shoulder, and my arms around his torso.

He clasped his hand atop mine and his heart while I swooned at how perfect he felt, how delicious he smelled.

"She broke something inside me." Aiden's voice wavered, and I hugged him tighter, wishing I could take all his pain away.

"You aren't broken, Aiden," I assured him, reveling in the heat of his body caressing mine at the points where we made contact. My groin sat well away from his back, thank God.

"She had an affair."

Shit. I clenched my eyelids shut. Having counseled a few married couples in the church after Zeke had left the year before, I'd heard my fair share of how infidelity could ruin a person's self-esteem. And a virile man like Aiden? One who didn't have faith to cling to? His ex was definitely the person who'd caused that emptiness in his eyes I'd seen.

"I'm glad you came home," I told him rather than asking for more information that would only drag up more distasteful memories of his I didn't need to hear—and he didn't need to relive.

"So am I." He exhaled heavily and squeezed my hand. "You've been a good friend, Padawan."

I let out a soft laugh. "I'm not a kid, Aiden."

"I know." His voice rasped, hinting at dangerous territory.

Tension rose between us in the immediate silence that took over my bedroom. Awareness of his citrus scent, the muscles I held radiated through my cells, bringing forth every lustful thought, every ounce of need my body could rouse to life within seconds.

I began to back away, but Aiden clutched at my hands.

"Not yet. Please."

Slowly releasing a leaked exhale, I stayed put, trying to not tremble.

"I meant what I said about how you're messing with my head," Aiden stated quietly, his torso as tense as mine.

I believed him, but I didn't know how to respond because of the hope/horror war still raging in my head.

"You give me a sense of home, more than California, my ex-wife, even my old job did."

I swallowed hard, unsure of how to deal with the

openness he showed by revealing the deepest part of *him*.

"Other than what you do to my dick, you make me feel more comfortable than anyone ever has."

A bite on my tongue kept my groan inside. I, weird geek, turned Aiden on. Lust to fulfill both our desires hit me harder than any shot of adrenaline "I'm sorry?" I offered what I wasn't sure he wanted to hear.

"I'm not. I like how you affect me."

"I've never liked how you made *me* feel." I gave him the brutal truth which caused him to chuckle.

"Liar. You loved when I walked around your parent's house without my shirt on. You *still* do. You always popped a boner if I accidentally on purpose brushed against you just to see how you'd react."

"Bastard," I muttered even though my heart rate matched the throb in my groin. I should have pulled away, insisted he let me go, but again, I soaked in every second I could of having Aiden in my arms.

He rubbed a thumb over the back of my hand still atop his heart. "Do you know how often I wonder if you have a pretty little dick, wildcat?"

"Fuck." I hissed at the sudden pain in my groin. "You can't say shit like that, Aiden."

"Two curses." Aiden made a tsking noise even though I could hear his smile.

I attempted to put distance between us again— and Aiden allowed it. Scrambling against my headboard, I grabbed my pillow and covered the obnoxious tent in my dress pants I hadn't yet changed out of.

Our gazes latched, and I held my breath, unable to move, same as graduation night when Aiden had read clear through to my soul.

"Let me see," he whispered, but I knew he asked what hid beneath the pillow rather than the emotions storming in my expression already laid bare to him.

I shook my head vehemently, too turned on, too off-kilter by the situation I found myself in to speak.

Aiden slid his gaze off my eyes, tracing every inch of my face and lingering on my lips. The pulse throbbing in my neck. Down over my askew tie and the top two buttons I'd popped open on my drive home.

Every muscle in my body tensed with the desire to spring toward him, tackle him onto my bed, and have my filthy way with him.

14

———————

AIDEN

I could taste Jed's desire, could feel it in pulsing waves coming off his tensed body. Imagining the mess I'd caused in his mind made me feel like a selfish piece of shit, just like my ex had often accused me of being.

But I wasn't, and I refused to put my own wants above what he needed. I cared too much about our friendship to screw shit up.

I ran my hand over Jed's foot with its thin sock. He gasped but didn't pull away.

"Your feet are cold."

"Always," he croaked.

Ignoring the discomfort of the massive hard-on in my pants, I got off his bed and went to his bureau.

Sure enough, he had a couple of pairs of fuzzy socks in the top drawer, and I grabbed his favorite

Boba Fett ones he'd worn to my place the last time he'd been over.

I felt his stare on my dick when I returned and settled closer to him, wishing he would just reach out and touch me. Put me out of my goddamn misery.

But he didn't. Jed wouldn't ever make the first move.

His breaths came heavy and shallow as I peeled off his thin socks. "What are you doing?"

I grasped his ankle, running my hands over his chilled feet. "Warming you up."

Jed swallowed hard while I eyed his toes. Perfect little digits, nicely trimmed nails. Soft against the pads of my fingertips. I wondered how they would taste—

"Aiden." Jed clutched the pillow atop him, his pupils blown and lips parted.

Fuck, I wanted to eat him alive.

Teeth clenched, I slowly replaced his thin dress socks with fuzzies.

"There." I squeezed both his feet and focused on his face again to find his expression unchanged. Crushing hard and hot for my touch. "Now your piggies won't be cold anymore."

Jed didn't look away, and I clearly read every bit of turmoil in his eyes.

His desire—for me, for his God. Doing what he

wanted as compared to what he thought was right as an ordained man.

I ought to feel guilt for causing his unrest but couldn't if it helped him find true happiness someday. "I'm not sorry," I repeated.

Jed surprised me by rolling his eyes. "My mess at this moment isn't about *you*, Aiden."

I tilted my head to the side to better see his face, but he'd gone back to his usual avoid-Aiden's-eyes game of old. He hid something, I realized. Prying might piss him off, but I couldn't help myself. "What's going on, Jed?"

He bit his lip while studying the pillow he still clutched to his lap that my fingers itched to yank away. I really lusted to see him—all of him.

"Come on, spill," I pushed when he didn't speak. "I just told you something about my ex that no one else knows—not even my parents. I'm pretty sure you can share whatever is going on in that head of yours."

Jed paused in his breathing before releasing a heavy exhale. A slight nod let me know I'd gotten him to cave.

"There are some...things going on at the church. Serious shit that if found out could cause major issues, and I'm torn about what to do."

"What shit?"

Lips tight, he stared at his lap.

"Welker's fucking his secretary?" I suggested the first guess that came to my mind.

"No, he's not fucking *our* secretary, Renee."

"Isn't she your mom's best friend? The one who used to hang out at your parents' house when we were younger?"

"Yeah," he muttered. "She got married and quit coming over not long after you left though."

"Welker's fucking one of his board members?" I guessed again, and even though they were all male I expected, I wouldn't put it past him.

Jed's head jerked back up. "Why do you think it's Welker?"

"Because he makes my skin crawl. Seems shady as fuck." I shrugged, but Jed's dark, expressive eyes said it all. Welker had indeed been up to no good. "Want to talk it out?"

He shook his head. "I'm...dealing with it, trying to figure out how to clear up the issue."

"A misunderstanding?" I *had* to push when he didn't trust me even after how I'd poured my heart out to him—uncovering the things I hated about myself the most.

"I don't think so, no."

I wracked my brain over what shit the man could be up to that could cause "major issues." If it wasn't fucking around...

I remembered the pastor's bullshit about giving until it hurt that he'd been talking about earlier when the offering had fallen short of the church's needs.

"It's money," I stated with assurance.

Jed blinked at me, his expression blank.

"Nailed it, didn't I?"

The war in his head intensified if his stormy eyes were any indication, so I patted his foot again, my curiosity sated. For the time being. "We don't have to talk about it anymore if you don't want to."

"Thanks," he whispered.

"But this…" I waved a hand between us, ready to get to all the shit I'd spilled via text.

"I don't want to talk about that either," he rushed to say before I could continue.

My shoulders slumped. "Why not?"

"I thought I'd made a decision for God right before you came over, but the second you're in my personal space after everything you texted me…I just don't know."

I definitely got to him, but I needed clearer definition. Hoped our desires would align so I could help him bust out of his goddamn prison.

"You don't know what?" I asked.

"What the truth is!" He shot out, his voice rising as though he was ready to finally lose his shit. "Right…wrong…why I want you—why I've *always* wanted you—what crossing those lines mean to me as a man, as a pastor—"

"Jed. Stop."

His mouth snapped shut.

Giving into self-indulgence—and needing an ego boost after sharing the shit of my ex—I crawled forward, lusting to yank Jed's slender form beneath me and push his weight into the mattress with my own. His mouth would yield beneath mine, I didn't doubt. His hands would grasp at my clothes, his whimpers more like fuel to the fire already burning inside me.

But even if he gave in to me, I would only be a disappointment, ruin his first time. Dash all his built-up dreams to wreckage.

His eyes widened as I caged him in without touching an inch of his trembling body.

"We can talk about it when you're ready, okay?"

Dumbly, he nodded, gaze still latched onto my face inches away from his as though I held all the cards, the lifeline keeping his heart beating.

A pregnant moment, a heavily charged silence, lingered between us. We shared breath, both our lips parted. The black of his pupils ate at the brown surrounding them, the pink high on his cheekbones a beautiful shade of embarrassment and need I wished I could fulfill.

The energy rippling between us could have lit a thousand lightbulbs. Goosebumps sprang to life over every goddamn inch of my skin. I wanted Jed with a deep yearning I'd never experienced before.

At that moment, I would have given him anything.

Everything.

But the hesitancy in his eyes let me know he wasn't ready—and strangely, I felt relief rather than disappointment after all we'd shared.

"Don't keep me waiting too long, Jed Simpson, or I might spontaneously combust." I backed off with the teasing words to cover my own torn mind, and he let out a rushed exhale.

"Bastard," he muttered a whisper that stretched my grimace to a grin, despite the ache in my groin.

"If you think my passivity is a temptation, you'd better gird your loins, Padawan. The issues between us?" I motioned between my straining dick and that goddamn pillow he clutched. "They've only just begun."

Obsessed didn't describe how I felt, and I was selfish enough to keep poking at Jed to get a rise out of him even though I doubted I would ever be able to fulfill his fantasies.

Shannon had made sure of that.

"I hate you!" Jed hollered at me as I disappeared from his sight, my focus on getting my ass out the door before I did something stupid like leap over the line he wasn't ready for, one that would reveal my shortcomings and probably cause him to feel regret I refused to allow.

"No, you don't!" I hollered back and chuckled the rest of my short walk home even though my heart ached as much as my balls.

15

____

JED

"One taste was all it took."

I sat enraptured by Mr. Williams's love story, vivid scenes playing in my mind as he shared —again—how he'd met Jonathan.

Similar to my first sighting of Aiden.

From afar, but an instant draw like magnets meant to stick to one another.

I could feel it in every cell of my body with vivid, tingling clarity when Aiden entered a room. When he'd touched me with his knee beneath my parent's dining room table. When I'd wrapped my arms around him, wanting to offer comfort.

When he'd suspended his body inches from mine, tempting me to taste the forbidden.

We would fit like puzzle pieces, and my heart and body screamed their truth when we'd claimed that what lay between us had only just begun.

But God...

I rubbed my temples, wishing I could curse my mom and dad for raising me in the church. Had I been led in the way of heathenism, there would be no agonizing decision.

Just living. Fulfillment I'd never felt in choosing God.

"Jonathan was my favorite man on the entire earth."

Lifting my focus off my shoes, I met Mr. Williams's watery blue eyes. My heart broke at the grief and longing on his weathered face.

"Do you believe you'll see him again someday?" I asked.

"Even faith can't give us that assurance."

There was no evidence of attack in his words, and the truth he spoke rattled around inside me. I once more appeared fascinated with my dress shoes, thinking about my later years and not having any memories to see me through the loneliness Mr. Williams dealt with.

Emptiness was all I had to look forward to.

"Who is he?" Mr. Williams asked quietly.

My shoulders slumped, my eyes falling closed. Longing to spill my guts and spew out all the built-up stores of anxiety inside hit me like a shot from Han's blaster pistol. What could it hurt by telling someone who didn't know my family, a man who had no connection to my work?

Someone who would understand.

Not judge me.

"My brother's best friend," I whispered, my voice ragged and low. Releasing the truth brought a sense of peace to lighten my burden but doubled the sting of my misery.

"How long?"

Eyes stinging, I huffed an agonized laugh, knowing I had no choice but to answer in a way Mr. Williams would understand. "Always."

I gave him my focus and immediately wished I'd kept my mouth shut for the intensified sadness in his eyes.

He held out his hand.

I took it, squeezing his bony fingers tight.

"Love is the most powerful force on earth," he told me, his tone firm for a ninety-seven-year-old man, full of assurance from having lived surrounded by what he spoke of.

God *is love.*

I pushed against the words I'd been fed for thirty-four years, wishing the only force was the kind from Star Wars. A simple drawing of energy from all living things around us, a welling spring of power for the body and mind.

"Love is the connection of souls," Mr. Williams continued, "and when you feel it for the first time, there's no denying its might."

I'd experienced it at fourteen.

Not once for anyone else.

Not when choosing the ministry.

Not when dedicating my life to the Holy Spirit's leading.

Every Christian I knew had at one point in their lives experienced God's presence in one way or another, and I'd often assumed it was the gay part of me that kept true communion from occurring between us.

I'd dealt with guilt for encouraging those hurting and worrying to pray and trust God, to live by faith in what He had planned, when I struggled to do so.

The one and only connection I'd felt similar to that Mr. Williams spoke of was with Aiden.

I wanted to burrow beneath his skin so there was no line drawn from where he ended and I began.

"It's a closeness more intense and beautiful than what we share with family," Mr. Williams said. "More potent than blood or friends could ever be."

I found myself wondering if I would ever enjoy the same, if I had the balls to consider doing what he'd done.

"That first taste?" He smiled, a little light cracking through the darkness of grief. "The love and acceptance of my parents and siblings could never compare to what Jonathan brought to my heart."

"No regrets?" I asked, searching his face.

"Not a one."

I headed toward Blackstone's Senior Living lobby exit, ready to crash and burn. Envy for the full life Mr. Williams enjoyed twisted my insides, adding to the mess of my head, and I just wanted to pass out and get some true rest.

Lay down, close my eyes. Sink into nothingness.

"Pastor Jed!" The director's call pulled me up short, and I turned, my smile coming without an ounce of energy.

I shook Mrs. Jackson's outstretched hand, her wide grin a flash of pearly white against flawless, unlined ebony skin even though she approached retirement.

"I wanted to thank you for sitting with Mr. Williams these last few weeks. We've seen such an improvement in his mood." She continued to hold my hand, her other coming atop mine, but I didn't mind the closeness. Mrs. Jackson embodied motherly instinct and caring, and I'd never felt anything but comforted by her presence.

"He's been a delight to spend time with." I spoke the truth of my hours spent with Mr. Williams.

She peered into my eyes, tempting me to glance away, but I held firm. "It's such an encouragement to see a man of God love in the way the Bible commands these days. Without preaching fire and brimstone or judgment."

"You're referring to the fact I don't condemn his sharing a life with another man," I stated bluntly, same as I'd always been able to do in my twenty-plus years of volunteering at Blackstone beneath her administration.

"Yes." Mrs. Jackson finally released my hand and gave me back my personal space. As a highly empathetic person, she clicked with a part of me that few did.

"You light up the lives of so many people in this building, and you have no idea how much I've wanted to beg you for more of your time."

"I wish I had it to give," I stated what I'd often thought myself. Spending Tuesday afternoons with the elderly, caring for their emotional and spiritual wellbeing, had been the most fulfilling thing of being in the ministry.

And the volunteering wasn't even part of my job at Simply Grace.

"I was hoping to grab you before you left. We have a new resident as of this morning, and I think she would benefit greatly from a visit with a soothing soul such as yours."

Soothing soul—something I'd heard her call me countless times in the years we'd worked together.

Even though I would have preferred to spend my hours with Mr. Williams, I knew others in the home enjoyed my company, perhaps even needed my empathy and ear.

"I'll be sure to visit with her first next week," I promised.

Mrs. Jackson wrapped me up in her arms, reminding me of Gram, even smelling like the same lilac perfume. "You're a good man, Pastor Jed. Blackstone is blessed to have you."

She would still consider her words to be truth even if she knew the hidden parts of me. I relaxed into her hold, allowing my mind a moment's rest in the assurance of her full acceptance.

If only my ministry at Simply Grace could mirror that of my volunteering at the nursing home.

There would be no choice, simply living.

No battle in my head.

Normal tiredness rather than the type of exhaustion that made crawling from bed every morning a chore.

I wished I could sleep and never wake.

16

AIDEN

I took on more graphic design side jobs to keep me busy, but when not at the gym or designing online, I pulled out my newest sketchbook and set to work on those characters I'd created with Jed in mind.

Two young lovers, both male, the push and pull between them evident in every scene I drew.

Ten images, hours poured into each, and still, my inspiration behind the couple hadn't seen them.

For three days, I allowed Jed room to breathe, to figure out the shit at the church. I would have offered to help in whatever way I could if only he had opened up to me with the truth of what Welker had done.

But he wanted to cover the sins of the spiritual authority in his life, that much I expected from having spent a few years in the same church. Welker had taken the pulpit while I'd been in California, but in one service, I'd read his bullshit for what it was.

Fake smiles, manipulative rhetoric, edification that people soaked up—fucking swallowed without thought—because of his place as "God's man."

Again, maybe I'd been too jaded, became too much of a think-for-myself type person, but I felt sure I could trust my gut about Simply Grace's pastor. Add in the trouble Jed hinted at, and I had no doubt.

Jed needed to ditch his job and find what made him happy.

Because it sure as fuck wasn't being an assistant pastor at that damned place where honesty and integrity were preached—and not practiced.

I stared at the last image I'd shaded gray and black, at the near kiss between the entwined characters. Lips parted, eyes closed. I could feel the tension between them, the same as had been between me and Jed on his bed Sunday after church.

"Should have kissed him," I muttered to the lifeless forms I'd created on paper. "At least Shannon hadn't ever complained about my skills in *that* area."

Maybe Jed's first kiss would shatter the wall he hid his true self behind. Maybe he did just need a sexual awakening to open his damn eyes to how perfect he was.

Maybe I need the same...

Blinking hard, I stood and made my way through the kitchen, my focus on the door and the hallway beyond.

Using the key he hadn't demanded I return even though I'd been a creep, I let myself into his apartment. Set my sketchbook on his table.

I second-guessed myself.

Instead of leaving all my drawings, I tore out a sheet and wrote a note telling him to call me when he got home—I had something I wanted to share with him.

Then I did go too far, stealing an item from one of his drawers because I had sick ideas floating around in my head.

I expected a call over the note I'd left, a text at the least, but a knock sounded a few hours later. Grinning, I yanked open my door, half-breathless without checking the peephole first.

"Jacob!" I stated his name a little too loud, my surprise evident with my dissolving smile. "Come on in."

He moved past me, and I shut the door after a quick glance across the hall. Had Jed gotten back from work? Had he stopped for dinner somewhere without texting me if I'd wanted anything like he'd done almost every night since I'd returned to Philly?

How badly have I fucked things up?

"That she-devil got to you, didn't she?"

I jerked around to find Jacob standing in the

kitchen, his arms crossed and feet planted. "Well, hello to you, old friend."

We hadn't seen each other since his family dinner the week before. He hadn't even reached out to me.

"I heard that you're designing the pamphlets for the family planning office over on Jefferson Street."

"And?" I had to poke even though I knew where he would go.

"Sixteen years ago, you took a stand alongside me and the rest of the Christian College Coalition at that pro-life rally. And now you're offering yourself, selling your artistic gifts to support the killing of innocent children?"

I wanted to light into him, to rip him a new asshole, but he'd become a zealot to his marrow. Arguing would be futile.

"I fear for your soul, Aiden," he stated sternly, his lips thinning.

I barely managed to keep from rolling my eyes. "Well, thank God for good men like your little brother who can pray for it."

Red flushed his face and not the sexy kind like the blushes Jed sported around me. "You stay away from him. I won't have you influencing him with your liberal ways."

"Jed is a man now." I hated I had to remind Jacob of that fact. "And—"

"He's God's man!"

"As I was *saying*," I drew the word out, my annoyance over being interrupted all too clear in my voice, "he can make his own choices, same as I do. Jed's life is his to live. He doesn't answer to anyone but himself."

"He answers to God," Jacob seethed, leaning toward me. I could imagine smoke rolling from his ears.

"The hell has gotten into you, Jacob? Huh?" I pushed, crossing my own arms and taking a stance he wouldn't be able to battle down. I was stubborn as fuck, and the few times we'd fought in the past, I'd always come out on top.

If he wanted to push, I wouldn't hesitate to push back.

"He's had a thing for you since childhood—sickening, but true, and now I've learned you're hanging out at Martin's every morning with Aaron and that pastor he lured away from the Lord!"

My insides burned. "Why, you homophobic asshole!" I hissed with barely restrained fury.

"I'm not a homophobe! I just follow God's word, and His truth states it's a sin. It's perversion!"

Homophobe.

"Do you rant at Jed like this?" I asked, my voice low—dangerous to my own damn ears. "Does that pastor of yours do so from the pulpit?" I asked, fully expecting I knew the answer—the reason for Jed hiding himself from family and friends.

"Of course, Pastor Welker preaches against sexual immorality!"

Fuck Jacob, fuck Pastor Welker, and fuck their church. A new truth of mine popped in my head, and I felt a smirk stretch my lips over the rise I was about to get from my old friend.

"I like dick too," I tossed out and waited.

Jacob's jaw dropped open, his eyes blinking.

Inwardly, I wanted to squeal with glee at the horror spreading over his face.

"Wh-what?" he rasped out, doubtless wondering how long I'd bent the bi way. If I'd wanted to touch *his* dick when we'd been teens and hadn't shied away from stripping down and redressing around one another.

I all-out grinned, letting him think what he would because I couldn't give two shits when it came to assholes like him who needed a good fucking sans lube with the sticks up their asses.

"Stay away from my brother," Jacob sputtered, recoiling back from me.

"I'd rather weasel my ass into his bed."

He blinked, the tension seeping out of his shoulders. "Aiden—please." I watched as pity, fear for my eternal soul, his love for his God broke through his fears. Jacob truly cared for me, wanted what he felt was best for me.

But that wasn't his faith or his Lord.

I wondered if it was his brother, but I was hesitant to allow myself that hope.

"I think it's time to agree to disagree, Jacob," I stated, uncrossing my arms to keep from seeming shut off. "We have a lot of history between us, a friendship I would hate to lose because of a difference of opinions."

"It's more than opinion to me, Aiden." His voice quieted, the look of anguish remaining on his face. "What you've chosen, how you're living now...its heartache and lashing out over losing Shannon."

He shook his head while my brain wanted to shout it wasn't a choice—it just *was*, same as Jed's innermost being.

"But it's toxic for me, and I can't have that in my life," Jacob continued. "You need to find the Lord again, Aiden. He's your only hope."

I almost spouted off a Star Wars line about Obi-Wan being our only hope, knowing Jed would have laughed, but managed to keep my sarcasm in check.

"Then I guess you should leave." No anger lit my tone, but I also meant the words with intent. Turning to open the door for Jacob made my desires crystal clear. "I'm sorry it's come to this, Jacob, but I think this is where we part ways."

He didn't respond but stepped back out into the hallway. "I'll pray for you."

"Don't bother." I shut the door and went straight for my cell in my bedroom, my insides tight and lips in a scowl even though my heart ached over the loss of my friend.

Don't answer the door, I texted quickly while walking back through the kitchen.

Wildcat: **Why not?**

Me: **It's your brother.**

Sure enough, a muffled knock sounded out in the hallway.

Me: **He's on a godly quest to condemn sinful souls to hell and break up relationships.**

The knock came again, and I peered out the peephole, watching the back of Jacob's dark head as he stood in front of Jed's door.

"I saw your car out in the parking lot," Jacob called loud enough I could hear his every word. "I know you're home." He dug his cell from his pocket when his brother didn't open up. For a few seconds, he hunched over, and I wondered what words they exchanged through text.

Shaking his head, Jacob finally turned and stalked off.

Me: **You okay, wildcat?**

Jed sent a red, angry face along with, **My brother's an asshole.**

I snorted on laughter while texting him back. **You're just now realizing that fact?**

He didn't reply, and I once more felt that sense of loss in my chest.

Me: **Want to come over and talk about it?**

Wildcat: **No.**

Me: **Why not?**

Three dots appeared. Disappeared. Appeared again.

"Come on, Padawan, give me something," I muttered, my blood starting to pool low in my groin and easing the anger I felt toward Jacob. "Anything. Please, man, I'm getting desperate over here."

His response when it finally came caused a groan to roll past my lips.

Wildcat: **Because I can't trust myself around you.**

My hands shook as I texted back. **Do you want to see what you do to me?**

Wildcat: **No!**

Me: **You do, trust me.**

Wildcat: **NO DICK PICS!**

Me: **You perv!** I attached a laughing emoji.

A quick pic of my sketchbook's final drawing crossed through the cyberspace separating us—the very thing I'd wanted to show him and had left the note about on his kitchen table.

Seconds later, a knock sounded.

I used the peephole that time and yanked open the door to find dark eyes peering up at me. Not having seen him for a few days, I soaked in the sight of his rumpled hair and flushed cheeks, my fingers itching to caress both.

"Let me see it."

I thought about making a lewd suggestion and grabbing my junk but refrained. "Told you," I said instead with a grin while stepping out of his way and allowing him into the devil's lair.

Jed strode into the living room, well aware of where I kept my artwork on the coffee table.

I shut the door—locked it in case Jacob came back—and ambled along behind Jed, enjoying the sight of sweats hugging his little but bitable ass.

He bent over the coffee table to pick up my book, just enough to stretch the cotton over his backside and make me swallow a groan.

Jed collapsed onto the couch, his gaze riveted on the picture of my boys a breath away from sharing a kiss. I rounded the edge of the couch and studied Jed where he sat, his face a luscious shade of pink, lips parted. The tip of his tongue peeked out to touch his upper.

My dick swelled to full mast, and a quick glance to his groin let me know he experienced the same— from the drawing, from being with me.

Fuck, did I want him.

"You feel it, don't you?" I rasped out, unable to keep the sudden need I had to touch, to taste, from my tone.

"It's perfect," Jed whispered, his focus so intent on my drawing he didn't think to grab the couch pillow from beside him to cover up the slender, hard ridge between his thighs begging for attention.

My mouth drooled to give it to him.

17

———

JED

Aiden had captured a million and one emotions with graphite and paper. Longing didn't begin to describe what coursed through my body. My balls ached, but I couldn't be bothered to tear my focus off the life Aiden had created to see how obnoxious my stiff dick had become.

"What's their story, Jed?" he asked quietly from where he stood towering over me, his tone as haggard as I felt inside.

"Forbidden love," I didn't hesitate to answer. "But they're powerless to fight it." The frown furrowed on one brow, the arched spine of the other in complete surrender to the one leaning over him... "It's beautiful. Simply perfect."

I imagined Aiden...

Back bowing to lift his body toward me. Searching

mouth, stuttered breaths. A moan of desperation rising from his chest.

Lips brushing, hearts tumbling as hunger takes over. Tongues and teeth devouring, hands desperate to mark heated skin. Bruising fingertips—bodies intertwining, becoming one heart, one soul.

Aiden let out a guttural groan, and I gulped, realizing I'd been speaking out loud.

Our gazes clashed, and I lost my ability to breathe.

He leaned down, and I sank back against the couch, the sketchbook forgotten on my lap. Hazel eyes pierced mine, more black than green as his warm breath moved over my mouth. "Jed."

My lungs stayed seized, unable to suck oxygen to feed my bloodstream.

"I want the same," Aiden whispered, and I closed my eyes with a whimper. "Look at me."

My eyelids shot back open.

And Aiden, my forever crush, the only man I'd ever allowed into my mind, my heart, pressed his lips to mine.

Dry and soft. A pillow I could relax into—but the tip of his tongue flicked the seam of mine, and I remembered how to breathe.

Need...more.

My blood rushed with a shot of adrenaline tightening my chest, my balls up against my groin, and I surged upward, grasping his neck in reckless abandon to the flesh.

His sketchbook thumped on the floor, and I shoved onto my knees, twisting him toward the couch beside me so I had access to every inch of golden skin covering his frame.

Aiden went willingly, sprawling on his back without our fused mouths breaking apart. The tongues and teeth I'd spoken of came into play, and I couldn't get enough. His exhales filling my lungs gave me life, swelling euphoria in every cell of my body even though I hadn't ejaculated. His tongue lashed at mine, curling my toes as I covered his body with my much smaller one.

Finally—I *finally* got to feel the muscles of him beneath me, every hard ridge and dip fitting perfectly against me. Butterflies lit throughout my entire core, straight to my chest, making me gasp for air.

He grasped my backside. "Jed," he groaned into my mouth, and my fingers speared into his hair to hold him in place so I could feast as I'd dreamed of doing.

I pulled while fumbling to taste every inch of his mouth, desperate for more...so much better than I could have imagined.

He tightened his hold and wrecked my mind with smooth, sensual glides of his tongue, the kind of first kiss I'd fantasized about.

And never expected to experience.

My pulse thrummed, making me light-headed as hell, and I clutched at Aiden's hair to keep my feet from floating off the ground.

"Jed," he whispered into my mouth again, his hips rising to press his hard length into my thigh.

My leaking dick strained against my sweats, attempting to dig into his lower abs.

Being shorter sucked—there would be no frotting unless he...

I tore my mouth off his and scrambled down his body until our groins touched, the need to touch him in that way more forceful than continuing to kiss him.

"Fuck." He held my gaze and clamped down on my ass to hold me in place while he lifted his hips, grinding us together.

I panted, gaze still stuck on his slack mouth that I wanted more of. On mine—my body—I needed—

His upper back lifted, his hungry lips giving me what I desired.

Yes...

Aiden pushed to sit, and my legs wound around his waist as though they belonged there.

Our dicks aligned, and his head lowered to reach my mouth. We moved as one, mimicking what I'd seen my favorite couple do time and again. Connecting. Giving. Loving.

My hole clenched at emptiness rather than the

thickness I rutted against. I wanted Aiden inside me. Filling me as I fucked myself down onto his length—

My balls erupted without warning.

I grunted, grasped at Aiden's head, and shuddered through my climax. He swallowed every sound ripped from my lungs as harshly as the cum shooting from my dick, obliterating every thought in my head but him.

Aiden.

That deep groan rumbled his chest again, and he yanked me close with a vise-like grip. He shuddered. Whimpered my name against my mouth as I soaked in his warmth, the perfect feel of his arms around me.

He'd come too I realized, my euphoria doubling.

We panted against each other's lips. Endorphins hovered me high atop an emotional mountain...one of my fantasies fulfilled, and better than anything I'd felt or fantasized about in my life.

Having gone from a frenzy of need to pure rapture, I blissed out, resting in the lap of luxury.

And hell, how perfectly I fit there on his powerful thighs, his hard chest and pecs warm against my cheek, his heart thumping in my ear.

In that moment, nothing mattered but him and how he filled every one of my senses. I knew true peace. Contentment.

"Fucking hell, that was hot," he murmured, his tone rumbling beneath my ear. "Shooting off like a goddamn teenager without a touch to my dick. Fuck."

A shudder rippled through me at the thought of how much better it would be *with* touching beneath clothing. I closed my eyes, and Aiden shifted to gently tuck my face into his neck. His groomed scruff had made me tender around my mouth from our frantic kisses, but I moved my lips over the soft skin he'd put in front of me, delirious for another taste.

Pure citrus deliciousness, ball-tingling even though I'd emptied mine.

"Keep that up," Aiden murmured close to my ear, "and I'm going to strip you down and enjoy the hell out of your pretty little dick, Jed Simpson."

Said dick perked right back up at his promise, and I broke out in goosebumps.

I pulled back, putting some space between our mouths.

Aiden brushed the hair off my forehead with a tender caress. Not one ounce of regret lit his eyes but a softness that could easily entice me to give him everything.

My soul, my family be damned.

"Let's do it," Aiden whispered, stuttering my heart to a stop as I had a vision of our naked bodies twisting, twining together to create that one heart, one soul I longed for—the kind of closeness Mr. Williams had spoken of.

"Wh-what?" I gasped.

"Write this graphic novel."

I stared, processing his words, trying to work out what the hell he'd meant.

"We'll publish it together," Aiden continued, still searching my eyes. "Who gives a fuck if we don't make money? We'd be fulfilling your dreams."

And the waterworks sprung a leak. Physical release often meant high emotions for me, and I couldn't imagine what he suggested we do. Together. As a team.

I scrambled off his lap as quickly as I'd attacked him, trying to right my clothing—some sticky and uncomfortable as hell—same as I attempted to make sense of the bomb he'd dropped on me.

"Hey." Aiden grabbed hold of my hand and thread his fingers through mine, immediately stilling my hurried movements. His touch also eased the rising tide of unrest inside me. "You write the words. I create the artwork. What do you think?"

"I-I think you're out of your mind," I sputtered the words without thought.

"Why?"

"Because...I'm a pastor—I can't write...that sort of book."

But hadn't we just humped ourselves off together? Hadn't I just enjoyed the experience of a lifetime?

"Then we come up with a pen name and create magic together with less of a sexual context. Seriously, Jed...it's like our gifts are two pieces of a puzzle."

The same thing I'd always considered us to be.

I imagined our bodies in the same manner, and my groin didn't care about the wet mess I'd already made inside my sweats. "You're serious, aren't you?"

"Dead. Let's do it."

"And this?" I whispered, motioning between the two of us, same as he'd done to me that night of our near-kiss.

"I don't know, Jed. You tell me." His intense gaze insisted he hoped for the same as me, but I couldn't give what he wanted. No matter how much Mr. Williams's words enticed my heart into believing I would never regret leaving my family for the possibility of lifelong love. Sure, Jacob had been a complete asshole in trying to control my life and the company I kept, but my parents...Trish and the kids...

"Not yet." I put my fingertip over Aiden's lips as he opened them to push like he always did. "I don't know."

He nipped and licked before curling his tongue around the tip and sucking. I stared as his lips closed around my finger. The deep pull, the suction of his mouth, swelled me to full length, stiff and aching.

"Don't make me wait too long," he whispered upon releasing my finger from his hot mouth.

I grabbed hold of my bulge to keep from shooting off again like the untouched virgin I was.

"Need help?" Aiden asked, one of his eyebrows rising with the corner of his lip.

"N-no. I-I don't need help."

"That's right...you've got all those toys you can use instead of the warm, willing body in front of you."

"I threw them out."

Aiden blinked. "What?"

"The...sex toys. I-I tossed them in the trash."

"Shit." He frowned. "I was seriously looking forward to seeing how you put them to good use."

I squeaked like a damn girl, and his slow smirk, like the Cheshire Cat, tingled down through me clear to my toes.

"Guess I'll just have to buy new ones once you give in to the fact that this is going to happen."

Such confidence...while all I held was the fear of reaping what we might sow.

18

AIDEN

Jed and I decided on a young adult-type sci-fi graphic novel rather than the erotic one my drawings had inspired in our heads. I didn't care what characters I drew as long as I got to spend a few hours with Jed every night, working with our bodies close and heads even closer.

For once, I truly sought out patience, giving Jed time and space to decide what he wanted for us when I'd have preferred pushing to get what I lusted for.

The kiss we'd shared had been one hell of an awakening for me, and my obsession for Jed intensified to the point I couldn't eat, sleep, or dream without thoughts of him invading my mind.

Shower? Milk my balls dry imagining him beneath me.

Pumping iron? Envision him in short shorts like some of the guys wore and fighting off boners.

Lying in bed after we finished work for the night and he left for his own place? Out came the bear and his wildcat videos to feed my fantasies.

I craved Jed riding my dick. Bending over the couch and begging for me to fuck him harder. Up against the tile in my shower. Pinned to a wall with my hand around his neck.

Him on his knees.

Me on mine.

But I also went beyond the physical once sated, wishing for his kindness, his soft voice in my ears, the accidental touches of his skin along mine. I wanted them intentional, comforting like a soothing balm to sunburn...I desired those things about him even more.

His sweet nature that never put me down, the words of edification my soul soaked up like the dried out sponge it'd become. And his adorable weird, geeky ways that turned me inside out like a giddy twelve-year-old kid? I lusted for that every day times ten.

Home, I'd considered him, and the more time we spent together, the idea came to certainty in my heart.

No matter the outcome of our friendship, the sexual innuendoes I couldn't help but put out there to see him squirm and face flush, I would always be there for Jed.

Even if he chose to keep me at arm's length.

"Blackstone is looking to redesign their logo," Jed told me, catching me with his off topic as I attempted to draw the spaceship he'd envisioned for our teenage smugglers.

"Is that the nursing home?"

"Yeah."

I wanted to hate the damn place since Tuesdays he didn't get home until later, but the joy he found in listening to the old folks reminisce and unload always had him smiling when he did finally show up on my doorstep.

Especially old Mr. Williams who'd become a close friend even though quite a few decades separated them in age.

"Any idea what they're looking for?" Logos weren't usually my thing, but I didn't doubt my skills.

Jed explained their current logo, and I attempted to draw what he brought to life in my head. "Pretty close," he said, leaning into my space enough that our shoulders brushed while he glanced down at the sketchbook in my hands.

"Closer," I whispered, running my nose along his jawline.

He jerked back to his side of the couch, face red.

"*Not* closer," he corrected me. "Something new. Fresh."

"I can do fresh." I winked, and he rolled his eyes.

"Blue rather than the old green...a little more whimsical than modern like the one they've been using since I started volunteering."

"How long have you spent your Tuesday evenings there?"

"Since deciding on the ministry. I enjoy being there ten times more than Simply Grace."

I decided to not push but made a few notes about the logo instead. "I can do a few mock-ups for you to take along with you next week. That way your friend..."

"Mrs. Jackson."

"...Mrs. Jackson can check out my work and see if we'd be a good fit."

"Thanks." Jed flashed me a quick grin but glanced back to his laptop just as quickly. "Do you think Xander and Zebin should get caught before attempting the run or drag out the chase a bit so they're closer to home? I think we could build more tension with a near-escape."

"Drag it out a bit, get readers' hearts racing and thinking they escaped with the shipment of...what'd they steal again?"

"The Chorindal's radiation converter. Remember how their world's core is toranium, and when they began to filter—"

Jed got lost in the fantastical world he'd created, and I gave up trying to understand, instead enjoying the excitement on his face, the rare use of his hands as he spoke.

His dark eyes lit with inner light, pure joy I'd only seen inside him since we'd decided to pursue his dream. I had no visions of grandeur, no hope of hitting any top sellers. I simply wanted to watch Jed bloom, using his gift to find peace and contentment.

"What?" He cut off his monologue.

I realized I stared—with probably a goofy grin on my face since that's how my insides felt. "I love seeing you happy, Jed."

Pink fused his cheeks, and he focused back on his laptop, his fingertips finding their placement.

"What else makes you happy?" I asked, insatiable for all things Jed.

"Coming home to sweats after a long day in a suit and tie."

"You're hot as fuck in a tie."

Jed shook his head but wouldn't look at me.

"What else?"

"Pineapple and ham on my pizza."

"Yes," I groaned the word, my stomach rumbling since it hadn't been fed in two hours.

More red spread over Jed's face. "Fluffies—you know I can't find my favorite Boba Fett socks. I can't even remember the last time I wore them."

My turn to focus on the work in front of me.

Guilt tingled the base of my spine, creeping into my consciousness, but I tucked it away for another day.

Those socks of his had gotten a lot of action. It turned out I had a thing for Jed's feet, something I'd never have considered kissing...toes worth sucking... but bear loved on wildcat's in a newer video they'd uploaded the week before.

Fluffy socks paid the price for my new foot fetish.

I cleared my throat, forcing away thoughts of being allowed to touch Jed whenever the hell I wanted.

"What else do you like, Padawan?"

"I can tell you what I *don't* like."

"Nicknames that make you feel like a kid?"

"Nailed it."

Lifting an eyebrow, I shot him a glance, staring at him until he finally looked up at me. "You can't use a one-liner like that and not expect me to think about having you beneath me begging for my dick, Jed."

He swallowed hard and jerked his focus forward. "I ought to go."

"No." I grabbed hold of his thigh when I'd have preferred to wrap my hand around his neck and kiss him senseless—since I knew I could. Fuck, what an ego boost. "Please stay. I promise I'll be good."

Lips tight, he nodded, and I released my hold on him, wishing I could show him exactly how good I could be.

Lousy.

My eyes clenched shut at Shannon's echo, and I shook my head to rid my mind of her vile words. A shudder wracked through me—I'd gone so fucking long without hearing her...

"Aiden?"

"Trying to keep my hands to myself." I caught his gaze and smiled but without any smolder, any hooded eyes to suggest lust since Shannon's voice had ripped those feelings from me. "You know what makes me happy? You, Jed. You've become my best friend—you're my favorite person."

Jed's eyes hazed over, and he once more played his don't-hold-Aiden's-gaze game.

I wanted to wrap him up in my arms, tell him he had worth outside of the life he'd lived for sixteen years, that he needed to step outside his comfort zone and take a chance.

Say yes instead of no.

But I wouldn't push.

I cared too much to worsen whatever issues clambered in his mind. The best I could do—be his partner in crime. Show him where he ought to find and latch onto his joy.

Without anything sexual that could cause the type of guilt and remorse that would tear us apart.

19

JED

For two weeks, Aiden and I worked late into the night, mapping out a storyline and learning the characters we created together.

It was pure magic sitting close beside him, soaking in the warmth of his body even though we didn't touch beyond an accidental brush of fingers or knees beneath the table.

He showed more restraint than I had expected after I'd given into my sinful nature and we'd crossed an ethical line.

Sure, he flirted, took every opportunity to toss out sexual innuendoes to make me squirm, but he kept his hands and mouth to himself.

While I lusted for both to the point I couldn't think straight.

Add in the rising tension in my guts from the church, more evidence from Jamie after the collections the next two Sundays that made the discrepancies in numbers very real, and I stressed to the point of missing another family meal.

Jacob texted me, questioning my absence, but I used the same excuse I'd given Mom—upset stomach.

While true, such a small discomfort wouldn't have usually made me avoid my mom and dad's house. The warnings to stay away from Aiden, the demands to not encourage his liberalism with my fleshly desires only soured my thoughts toward my brother.

He'd always been the one to stick up for me, the one I'd looked up to. The one whose life I'd envied. But with every day that passed and every negative word from his fingertips on my cell screen, I realized our relationship approached a line that once crossed, wouldn't be salvageable.

If you loved and cared for someone, you built them up rather than spewed Bible verses in attempts to "help." You lent a hand, offered a shoulder to lean on, listened when your loved one needed to be heard.

I had no one to share my secrets with outside of who they centered around—but I knew a man who must have experienced what I battled over in my brain.

I hadn't talked to Ezra since he'd left his job at Simply Grace for Aaron.

Having heard through the grapevine he'd begun counseling at a new LGBTQ home in Philly, I searched out Humanity House's number and used my cell at home where I wouldn't be overheard.

A sweet-voiced lady answered the phone and put me through to his number.

Ezra didn't pick up, but I left a short message, asking him to get back in touch with me.

A few minutes later, my cell rang with an unknown number, and fingers crossed, I answered.

"Jed, it's Ezra," he said, his rich baritone voice like a soothing balm I hadn't realized how much I'd needed.

"Hi. Sorry for bothering you at work," I said, sinking onto my couch.

"A call from a friend is never bothersome."

My throat tightened at the word friend even though we hadn't known each other that long—and hadn't spoken to one another in what felt like even longer. "Thank you."

"How can I help?"

Always so giving, same as he'd been those brief months we'd worked together at Simply Grace Church, I was blown away by his graciousness. It was no wonder Aaron loved him as he did.

"I'm having difficulty...with personal matters, and I needed someone outside the church."

"I won't offer you spiritual guidance, Jed," Ezra

stated quietly, and I nodded even though he couldn't see me.

"I know—but that's not what I'm looking for right now."

"What do you need?"

"An ear."

"Then you have mine," he promised, a smile in his voice.

"Are you sure you have time?" I asked, wiping my palm on my sweats. "It's kind of a long tale."

"I have a free hour—and I won't even charge you a counselor's fee," he joked, twitching my lips.

Starting at the beginning when I'd first met Aiden, I laid most of my past out on the table, only keeping my fantasies, toys, and favorite porn couple to myself. Ezra didn't interrupt, simply commenting on occasion to assure me he still listened.

I poured out my heartache, the longing I expected he would understand, and the war that battled constantly in my head until exhaustion weighed me down.

"Do you love him?"

"How can I not?" I half-laughed, tears lacing my voice. "He's the only man I've ever felt drawn to in this way, the only one I've ever dreamed of, the one I imagine spending my life with."

"Do you love God more?"

I couldn't answer.

Did I even look at God in the way the Bible

commanded us to? I'd sought His will out of habit since childhood, and nothing had ever brought my choice into question before.

But Aiden's physical return to my life made me agonize over everything I felt, all I'd thought to be true.

"My mind is so full of conflicting emotions," I admitted, "and with the situation at the church compiled atop my personal issues, I'm unable to take any step forward. It's like my feet are stuck in cement, rooting me in desperation for answers and depression over God's silence and the possibility all I've known is nothing more than ashes in the wind."

"What's going on at the church?" Ezra asked, and I closed my eyes, lips pursed.

I had no issue uncovering my own sins, but possible ones of a man who shepherded a few thousand-plus member church and the day school my brother oversaw? Opening my mouth put Jacob's job at risk, but I'd reached the point where I couldn't shoulder the burden on my own with timid Jamie unable to hold me up.

"Nothing would surprise me," Ezra said when I still didn't answer, "and I also won't be the one to share what's going on."

"Even with how Pastor Welker treated you? With all the vile things he's said about you and Aaron?"

"Even then," Ezra assured me, his tone firm. "I am no longer preaching God's word, but I know what it means to be a real child of God—and outside my view on loving freely, I stick to His principles."

Ezra had showed Welker grace and mercy when he had every right to tear the man apart. He was a true Christian in every sense of the word as far as I was concerned.

"He's siphoning money from the offering," I whispered, my eyes clenched shut.

I didn't get a response.

"Ezra?"

"How long has this been going on?" he asked, his voice suddenly sounding tired, same as mine. Loaded with disappointment—also same as me.

"Jamie and I have been going through past spreadsheets and deposits, secretly meeting after work every Monday to check the numbers from the Sunday before. The discrepancies started over two years ago."

"Who else knows?"

"Besides Mr. Bowers, the treasurer who *has* to be involved, no one," I said, thinking of the various copies of evidence Jamie and I had made and hid away.

"Renee—she's still your and Welker's secretary?"

"She's blinded by her adoration of him and wouldn't ever consider he would do such a thing. Besides, you know how she can't keep her mouth shut. I'd have heard from my mom if Renee suspected a thing—they're best friends and have been for most of my life," I added.

Ezra let out a heavy exhale. "Does Welker have any idea of what you and Jamie are digging around in?"

"Not that I'm aware of, no."

"You're aware of the files he keeps, the pictures he has. I wouldn't put it past that man to have dirt on every single one of his followers—truth or fabricated. Especially the people on the board and his staff."

I remembered Renee's husband who didn't have anything to do with the church beyond attending every Sunday.

As the associate pastor, I would certainly be at the top of the list to have my sins ferreted out. But I'd led an outwardly holy life, only falling short behind closed doors.

"I'm not concerned in that aspect. Jacob, you, and Aiden are the only ones who know about the real me."

The real me.

Those words echoed in my head, loosening the cement-like hold on my feet.

Too much exhaustion and anxiety came from pretending to be someone I wasn't, and the knowledge I could easily break free if I wanted to swelled something up inside me.

"Just be careful, Jed. Call me if you need any help —anything at all."

I smiled, my heart lighter than it had been for weeks. "Thank you for being available, Ezra."

"Thank you for not judging me and my lifestyle."

If only he understood how much I envied what he had.

Reality, I whispered again in my head after hanging up. Why did I hold back being me—the *real* me? The person who'd been formed in Mom's womb? Being demisexual was just as non-*normal* as being gay in my church's eyes. It sickened me that some thought they had the right to decide right from wrong according to ancient teachings or their opinions built upon their parents as mine had been.

Theirs.

Not mine.

My life wasn't there's to control, theirs to live.

I hadn't ever once considered telling others which steps to take, even when doing counseling or visiting with the congregation's invalid and sick.

Speaking with Ezra had given me a bit of hope. While choosing to be me would definitely tear my close-knit family apart, I felt that there might be light awaiting me on the other side as Mr. Williams and Jonathan had found for seventy-plus years.

There were also friends I hadn't realized were rooting on the sidelines.

Ezra had found peace. Zeke had as well.

They both used their gifts to minister to hurting souls, just not to the godly-minded individuals who chose to worship Him.

Chewing on the inside of my lip, I decided I needed to at least tug one foot from the cement and take a step on my own.

Test waters by partaking in a bit of unholy temptation.

I picked back up my cell and called Aiden, surprised by my clear conscience.

20

———

AIDEN

Wildcat's name popped on my screen, his *Wild Thing* ring tone sending a rush through my blood.

"My favorite man," I answered with a grin.

"Want some company?" Jed asked, his words rushed and breathless.

It sounded like he was looking for more than someone to hang with, but I refused to get my hopes up. I'd decided to give him his space and time to get shit straightened out, but I wasn't counting chickens before those fucking eggs got their shit together and hatched.

Preferably on my lap.

"Pizza and *Firefly*?" I suggested.

"Be over in a bit."

"I'll put in the order."

Still grinning, I did as promised. I pulled out

some plates and napkins and set my sketchbook and the graphic novel stuff we'd been working on to the side of the coffee table we preferred to eat at.

The pizza showed up first, and I shot off a text one-handed to Jed to hurry his ass up while shoving a piece in my mouth.

Ham and pineapple—could anything be more delicious?

Jed.

My dick twitched in agreement, and I realized I hadn't gotten in my pre-Jed arrival jerk-off like I'd been doing every night the previous couple of weeks. Tented shorts it would be. Maybe having something to look at would entice Jed to let loose. Allow that wild kitty he kept under lock and key out to play.

But then I'd be faced with trying to please him.

The voice in my head assured me I wouldn't even though my kisses had been enough to help him get off what seemed like ages ago.

Fucking Shannon.

I still frowned while licking grease off my fingers and answering Jed's knock with my other hand.

The second my door unlatched, it shoved inward. An oomph flew from my lungs as a body hit mine.

Jed climbed me like a goddamn tree, and I grabbed his perfect ass, yanking him fully against me. My heart pounded in my chest, threatening to break free.

A lash out of my foot slammed my door shut at the same time his mouth met mine, and I groaned at the sweet taste of him I'd fantasized about savoring over and over again.

So. Fucking. Delicious.

Small but mighty, Jed clung to me and attacked me with hands and lips, tongue and teeth, fumbling to touch every bit of my skin he could find in his desperation.

I wanted to slow the fuck down, enjoy the hell out of tasting every inch of him, but he rutted against me like an animal hellbent on busting a nut.

My dick throbbed with the same need, but I peeled him off my body.

"No," he whispered, hands grasping at my hair as he tried for my mouth again.

"Oh, I have zero intention of stopping this, wildcat," I assured him, breathless and horny as fuck for a full taste of his lithe body, "but slow down before we both erupt in our pants again."

"We have all night," he insisted, eyes wide and blown black, still grinding over my aching length.

Unless I proved a disappointment the first time around.

I licked his lower lip, nipping when he tried to take control of our kiss. "Let me taste you first, Jed. Please. I want your pretty cock in my mouth."

"Quit calling it pretty."

"I'll bet it is. Pink like your flushed cheeks." I rubbed my nose along his jaw. "Smooth like the skin on your face. Please." I wasn't above begging. Having a part of Jed inside me before striking out in the sack was as selfish a thing I could ask for—but I could try to make it good for him.

He loved my mouth on his after all. Maybe I would excel at giving head too.

"Yeah. Okay." He shimmied out of my arms as fast as he'd scaled my body, and I put a hand on his chest, pushing him against the wall.

Our gazes locked, my heart tripping at the emotion pouring from his dark eyes. Lust and longing rippled between us with an electrical charge, the type that raised the hair on my arms and nape.

"You're sure?" I whispered, afraid to push too hard and have him surrender to regret afterward.

"Get on your knees for me and suck my pretty dick."

A jolt struck my groin at his blunt command, and I damn near came. "Fucking *hell*, Jed." Swallowing hard, I stared at the man I thought I knew—and clearly didn't. "What the fuck was that?"

My question heightened the color on his cheeks, and he bit down on his lower lip. "Knees...please, Aiden. Touch me. Taste me." His voice had lost the firm tone to embarrassment, but he still stated what he wanted.

I gladly sank to my knees while holding this gaze.

"Take it out," I said, my voice rasped to hell. "Let me see."

His hands shook as he fumbled to yank down his sweats that didn't leave much to the imagination.

Slender and pink, exactly as I'd imagined, his dick slapped against his body once finally released from its prison.

"Jed." I ran the backs of my fingers up his length, eyeing the bead of moisture rising from my touch.

"Oh shit." He gulped, a shudder rippling down through his entire body.

"So pretty," I whispered.

"Little."

"Average," I corrected even if he was on the shorter side of mine. And the fact I had a bigger, thicker dick?

Made me feel like a damn bear. Gave my ego such a boost I didn't even *think* about letting him down.

Confident and pulse thrumming with anticipation, I replaced my fingertips with my tongue and licked him from drawn-up balls to frenulum.

I was the first and only man to taste him, his untouched body. A growl rose in my throat at the thought he belonged to me—only me.

His pre-cum oozed over the silken head, reaching my tongue, and Jed's taste exploded in my mouth, enticing my dick to leak too.

Who knew a guy's spunk would be so damn addicting?

I lapped it up, groaning and grabbing my base to keep from blowing in my shorts.

"So good," I murmured and closed my mouth over the head of his dick, sucking to pull more up through his slit.

"God...fuck, Aiden, just like that." Jed's fingers found my hair, tugging me closer. "I want to fuck your throat—I need to..."

I had zero experience at giving a blowjob, but I used my tongue how I'd want someone to worship me, fighting off my gag reflex when Jed shoved in too far in his urgency.

Wetness rolled down my cheeks every time I choked on him, but I ate that shit up, every whimper, every curse on Jed's lips making me feel like a damn god of cock sucking.

He has nothing to compare it to.

Shoving aside that thought, I pulled off his dick and moved lower, readying to give him another first.

"No—don't stop, please—" Jed's voice gave way to a guttural groan as I sucked one of his balls into my mouth. "Oh...oh, fuck, Aiden." He lifted onto his toes, holding my face to his groin, and I rolled his soft flesh over my tongue, suckling until he whimpered and my nuts seized up tight.

"I'm going to come," he gasped out, and I shoved my mouth back over his dick, catching every spurt on my tongue, struggling to swallow everything he gave me.

Curses hit my ears, my name along with them, tingling my balls with the need to release.

The second Jed sagged against the wall—his dick still hard, I sat back and yanked mine out.

Two strokes and roaring like a bear, I shot my load all over my hallway floor. Face buried in his groin, I sucked wind, my heart racing and my skin burning the fuck up. Jed's earthy scent filled my nose, and I rubbed my face all over him, uncaring that my saliva and remnants of cum smeared over my cheeks and mouth.

So. Damn. Delicious.

I shuddered, a final moan slipping past my lips, but couldn't move.

Jed sank down in front of me atop my spunk without a care, sweats around his crossed ankles.

Our gazes locked, and where I expected to find regret, I saw a blissed-out man with a gorgeous, flushed face.

"Okay?" I heard myself ask, my insecurities rising to the surface regardless of how hard he'd come or the encouragement and praise he'd rained down on me.

"The man of my every fantasy just sucked my dick and swallowed my cum without gagging at the taste—what do you think?"

"That good, huh?" I couldn't help but push with a grin, my chest swelling to its max.

"Better than good." His smirk faded, and he rubbed his thumb over my lower lip. "Divine. Earth-shattering. Axis-spinning. Inspirational."

"Keep going," I joked with a laugh, knowing I would never hear enough edification from his lips, my insides wanting to preen beneath the precious words he poured over my soul.

"Perfection."

Our gazes latched again. We both leaned forward at the same time, our mouths coming together but without the hurried lust from before.

Jed's fingers found my hair, and I pulled him sideways onto my lap, wanting him closer even though my cum sticking to his backside smeared over my thighs. His dick remained hard between us, and I couldn't help a few gentle caresses.

"What are you? The Energizer bunny?" I asked between kisses.

"It's just attempting to make up for lost time."

"Mmm." I sucked on his lower lip, nibbling until he released a ball-tingling moan. "I want more," I murmured, pulling back to judge his reaction.

"So do I," he agreed, his voice quiet, "but I think I need to process first?"

"Is that a question or are you telling me that's what you should do?"

Jed let out a heavy exhale, his sweet breath filling my lungs and making me want to take his mouth again regardless of his answer. "Telling."

"Okay." I forced myself to set him aside and kept my hands to myself rather than fully wrapping my fingers around his length and enticing him to let me watch cum spurt from his dick.

He stood, and I groaned at the short distance between his groin and my face. "You like this, don't you?" he asked, using his hand to adjust his dick toward me.

"Tease—but yes. A lot. More than I expected," I admitted, still sitting on my ass, my hands fisted in my lap.

"I expect I'll like yours too." Jed glanced at my chub. "Next time it's my turn for a taste."

Fuck, did I hinge my hopes on that statement.

We cleaned up, both of us lounging on separate corners of my couch after inhaling some pizza.

"So, what brought about your change of heart?" I asked in my usual nosey way, not sounding nearly as casual as I'd tried for. Giving Jed a few of his firsts had turned me inside out, and I struggled to focus on anything but claiming the rest.

"I spoke with Ezra."

"Bravo." I grinned, giving him a slow clap. "It's about time you got an outside voice to help you see reason and ease some of the tension riding you the past couple of weeks."

"I told him everything." Jed held my gaze while admitting it. "Well, not about my *secret* secrets."

"Toys and porn," I filled in as his face once more turned a luscious shade of pink.

"Yeah, those."

"Welker?"

Jed blew out a heavy exhale. "That too."

I wanted to get upset he didn't trust me with the entire church issue, but I expected Ezra would have a deeper understanding of Jed's turmoil. "And?"

"He told me to be careful. Welker...he keeps tabs on the people beneath him if you know what I mean."

Shady fucker. Didn't surprise me one bit. "How so?" I asked anyway.

"Files. Pictures. He confronted Zeke last year— and he took me along as a witness when approaching one of the deacons with images that proved he'd been unfaithful to his wife a few weeks after Ezra left the church."

"He probably has shit on everyone."

"He's been watching our secretary's husband too because—you'll never believe this one—he was seen going into the adult store across from Martin's."

"Are you fucking with me right now?"

"Nope." Jed shook his head. "Seriously. Who gives a flying fuck what a husband and wife do in their bed? For all we know, he could have just wanted some flavored lube because his wife doesn't like the taste of his dick."

I stared at Jed, listening to what he said, the words he chose. His first blow job had definitely shifted some things around in his brain to make him talk like that.

I'd done that for him—and I fucking loved it.

Smirking, I grabbed his fluffy-socked foot and set it on my lap, digging my thumbs into his arch.

The boring blue ones, I noted, only a slight twinge of guilt over stealing his favorites hitting my brain.

"I don't see how he would have anything on me since I've been such a damn saint, but what if he does?" Jed rubbed his palms down his sweats.

"Relax, kid. Unless he has hidden cameras in this apartment or yours, he doesn't have jack shit on you. You *have* been too much of an angel since childhood."

"I'm starting to think my whole life has been a lie."

Fuck, how I longed to push him to expand and see the truth on that one, but I bit my tongue. Jed coming to his own conclusions would settle facts in his head more firmly than my nudging ever would.

"What I want," he spoke slowly, "isn't fair to you, though."

"Nothing has ever felt better than this, Jed," I told

him my truth, allowing vulnerability when I rarely did. "You can tell everyone we're just friends. No one needs to know."

He allowed me to have his eyes for a moment while heat once more simmered between us raising the hairs along my arms.

"I live across the hall," I murmured, still rubbing the sole of his foot. "Call me whenever. Whatever you want, it's yours."

"Aiden," he groaned my name, and I squeezed his foot, recognizing the truth of my words in the deepest parts of my soul.

I might have found satisfaction in being the sole man to possess Jed in the way I had, but he owned my heart.

And nothing, no one, no higher being, would ever change that fact.

21

———

JED

Another week dragged by while I considered a second step from the cement and the conversation Aiden and I had before I'd left him after the hottest night of my life.

He didn't mind remaining my secret.

No one needed to know.

Whenever, he'd promised. Whatever I wanted.

His words buoyed my spirits, kept me from being pulled beneath the surface over all I faced—my future, my family, and my job.

I skipped service on Sunday, leaving Welker a voicemail that I wouldn't be there. I just couldn't sit on stage and listen to his lies. A text to Mom assured me she'd be stopping by with some soup later that afternoon.

Not attending church brought on the phone call I expected.

"I'm worried about you, Jed," my brother stated sternly. "You never miss church, never shut yourself off from the family like this. Is it the lure of sin?"

Lure of sin.

I held in my snort. He had no idea how that part of my life had somewhat notched into place. It was the foundation I'd based my entire existence on that shook me to my core.

"I'm not feeling well."

"It's Aiden, isn't it?"

I let out an exasperated sigh, hoping he caught my annoyance over the line. "No, it's not Aiden."

"Since he's come home, you've pulled away. The last two Sundays you've been at Mom and Dad's, you didn't smile a single time. Even my kids couldn't get you to crack your seriousness. Not even Johnny's new baby Yoda shirt."

I did smile at that one, not that Jacob could see. "I've just had too much on my plate lately," I went with a half-truth. "The church has a lot of illness going on right now, and I'm running myself ragged trying to visit hospitals, death beds, and suffering souls. It's starting to wear me down."

That final bit was an outright lie, but I pushed aside the guilt.

I wanted Aiden with bone-deep longing, but allowing myself to love him in the open would ruin all I'd clung to throughout my life, same as Mr. Williams's choice had done to him.

It had happened to Levi when he'd skipped town to be with Zeke, but he'd never had a good relationship with his parents to begin with. My family had always been close, and the idea of taking a chance with a man recently jaded, searching for his own path in life, didn't sit well in my gut regardless of how my heart screamed agreement with Mr. Williams.

I couldn't put Aiden from my mind no matter how hard I tried. Choosing him in that moment had set me free to be *me*, the person I'd been at birth.

We made magic together on paper—and the physical pull between us even more so. Like he'd said, nothing had ever felt better, and I wanted to take another step. Have another taste—

"I can sense you drifting away."

Again, I held in a snort. Jacob didn't spend enough time with me to know what I did or didn't do. I wondered where he got his inside information, but I hadn't shared an ounce of my struggles with Mom or Dad. Not even Trish when she'd quietly asked me the Sunday lunch before if I was okay.

I'd shrugged her off, same as I'd done with anyone seeming to show concern for my well-being.

"I'm not drifting away, Jacob," I said, hoping to hide the annoyance from my voice. He was still my brother, and I loved him regardless of his shortcomings.

He meant well.

"Even Renee told Mom you've been acting strange."

"Strange how?" I asked, hoping the spike of adrenaline through my system wasn't obvious in my voice.

"Quieter. Keeping to yourself and eating outdoors rather than in the church cafe like usual."

"I told you, I'm just tired." More lies. How long until I tripped up, causing a serious mess within my family?

"Aiden isn't the man he used to be, and I'm afraid all this time you've been spending with him is drawing you away from the fold."

Aiden isn't the kid you knew.

"Don't let him influence you with his liberal stance or tempt you to stray from a godly life."

"He hasn't."

More like I tempted him with how I'd thrown myself at him the night before. Attacking his mouth, tearing at his clothes to reach his skin.

Swallowing hard, I blinked the memory from my mind even though it filled me full to bursting with happiness and a desire for more.

"Imagine what Mom and Dad would think if you left the ministry to write your silly sci-fi books."

Books—wait. He wasn't referring to sexual perversion when he'd spoken of liberalism and taking a course other than living a life fashioned after God?

I frowned, sure I'd misunderstood. "What are you talking about, Jacob?"

"He told me you're writing again."

Aiden had shared our secret?

Disappointment struck like a knife, jagged and sharp to my heart.

"And while I understand you've always enjoyed your creative outlet," Jacob continued while I stewed over hurt and anger, "it's a hobby. Not sustainable. It also won't gain you the riches in glory like tending to His flock will."

Riches in glory—something Ezra had always striven for and had gladly exchanged for Aaron. Something I hadn't given much thought. Something that would never dictate how I lived.

I didn't, would never have the same dogmatism as my brother. I'd made a poor choice—the wrong decision—in pursuing Gramps and Grandpa's hopes for my future.

"You would have been a better pastor than I am, Jacob," I murmured the absolute truth while my insides struggled to deal with the hurt Aiden had caused.

My declaration caught Jacob's tongue.

"You rededicated your life to God and have a commanding presence I'll never find inside myself," I continued. "You're the shepherd out of the two of us."

He excelled at attempting to corral people

toward godliness while I simply chose to love people where they were in life.

"Stay in the word of God, Jed. It's the only book that matters," Jacob offered as a goodbye, but I didn't make any promises.

I hung up more annoyed than before he'd called and immediately texted Aiden.

Me: **You told Jacob about our secret.**

Aiden: **???**

Me: **The book.**

I hit send, my lips tight and my stomach in knots.

Aiden: **Oh...that!** His laugh emoji didn't crack a smile on my face. **I thought you were talking about how much you love my mouth on you.**

My dick didn't get the memo about being upset with the object of my obsession.

Me: **Jacob is all up my ass now over being led astray from my calling, assuming that's why I skipped church, so thanks for that.**

Aiden: **You skipped church and didn't invite me over?**

Me: **How about an apology for once? Or are you unable to think beyond your libido?**

I tossed my cell aside and hopped in the shower, hoping the hot water would clear the anger from my head.

Aiden had said we could write the book together and no one would need to know. We had agreed to keep what we did a secret even if it wasn't the gay erotica we sometimes joked about writing.

Because my family would frown on such going-ons that had nothing to do with God and everything with greed for earthly things.

My hands wanted to fist and punch Aiden. My tongue wept with the need to taste him.

"Shit," I muttered, hating the emotional rollercoaster I'd been caught up on.

A dark shadow shifted in my periphery, shooting adrenaline through my system.

Aiden stood in the bathroom doorway, arms crossed over his bare chest, shorts hanging low on his hips. "The fuck, Jed?"

My anger spiked again even as my dick roused to full life. Mentally, I cursed to no end.

I shoved open the shower door and grabbed my towel, not giving Aiden my attention. "I could ask you the exact same thing. Our secret—a pen name —we were going to accomplish my dreams without anyone the wiser. Do you remember why?" It was my turn to push, and I did, finally facing him with the towel wrapped around my waist as I got all up in his space.

He stood like a statue, unmoving as I poked at his rock-hard chest when I'd have preferred biting his skin...or beating on it while screaming.

"So I wouldn't have to deal with this sort of shit!

You know how close I am with my family, how they'll judge me!"

Aiden's arms dropped to his sides. "That's why you hide who you are."

"Fuck off," I muttered, shoving past him and heading to my bedroom.

I could feel him hot on my heels.

"It has nothing to do with God, His calling, your church—it's your family that keeps you from living your real life."

"This *is* my life!" I spun, my arms held wide, my heart pumping, all my emotions I'd bottled up for weeks rising like a can of soda shaken and ready to explode.

"And you're not happy!" Aiden shot back, his turn to get in my face, his head lowered, eyes dark and stormy. "You're squashing your creative genius. Your chance to love and be loved how you've always wanted. A partner, kids...fuck, Jed." His voice broke, but he pushed on. "I need those same things, and not getting them, having what I'd thought was the right path toward those goals ripped from me—"

Aiden's rant cut off on a choked sob, and he stumbled back two steps, his eyes hazed over with tears.

Shannon.

I moved in without thought for my own vulnerability, my anger toward him fizzled out by the pain in his eyes. Wrapping my arms around his torso, I hugged him, pressing my cheek against his bare chest. Warm. Hard. My eyelids fluttered closed.

His arms wound around me, pulling me in tight.

Skin on skin—the worst temptation at the least ideal time.

Wetness dripped onto my head, but Aiden made no noise other than to struggle with breath while I fought to control my throbbing dick he had to feel poking against his thigh.

"I'm so sorry she hurt you," I whispered, understanding his emotions beyond my need and wishing I could take it away.

"She was fucking someone behind my back," Aiden said, his voice shaky, choked up, as he fought off his emotions. "I had to go get tested, scared as fuck she'd picked up some disease and passed it on to me. I didn't touch her after getting cleared—not that she'd have wanted me even if I'd begged for reconciliation."

I hugged him tighter, my heart breaking as he let out a heavy sigh.

"I'm over it."

"You're not." I put some distance between our bodies and lifted my face to better see him.

Tear tracks lined his cheeks, but he didn't release my waist to wipe away the evidence.

"It's okay to feel broken, to feel lost."

"Like you are."

I nodded, realizing there was no point in holding

anything back from Aiden since he'd told me the truth of why his marriage had ended. "My world has turned upside down—same as yours. I'm struggling to find footing, to make sense of my heart, my head... it's overwhelming, and for the life of me, I can't choose. Do I confront Welker for his thievery? Leave it alone and trust God to deal with him?"

"Out his ass," Aiden muttered.

"Do I take a chance on the one and only man I've ever wanted and probably lose my family?" I asked, my voice lowered.

"One and only?" Aiden's eyes twinkled, heating my skin.

I dipped my focus to his chest and the dark discs of his nipples I wanted to lick. Bite.

Clearing my throat, I laid it all out. "No one else has ever turned me on. No male, no female...no one but you. Once you left, I labeled myself as asexual, but that can't be right since distance and time obviously hasn't dulled my attraction to you."

Aiden pulled me close again, sliding his leg between mine and causing the tightly wrapped towel around my hips to gape. His bare leg rubbed against my groin, taking me back to hard as granite with one quick inhale.

"Aiden," I croaked, my fingers digging into the muscles along his spine.

"Do you have any idea what that confession does to me, Jed?"

I could imagine—but I'd given him my thoughts. I deserved the rest of his, especially since knowing would allow me wisdom in helping to heal his heart. "Shannon put you down, didn't she? Blamed you for her choices."

"All the fucking time," Aiden snipped the words as his hands found my ass and he ground me against his hard thigh. "But you? You're like a blood transfusion, offering me life again. The things you say... knowing you've saved yourself for me...Christ, Jed."

My body buzzed with need. I smirked at his assumption I hadn't done *anything* before him—but he spoke the truth. I'd only ever desired for Aiden to have all my firsts.

"I'm scared as fuck to disappoint you."

My head shot up at his confession, and the wariness in his eyes made me want to hug him even harder. *Fucking Shannon.* "You could never."

"I did—telling Jacob you were finally writing again."

"You meant *sexually* with that disappointment comment, Aiden. Don't change the subject back to what started this much-needed conversation."

He nodded, searching my eyes. "I didn't explain what you wrote, Jed. I wouldn't ever reveal your secrets like that. I'm just so damn proud that you've taken a step toward inner happiness, doing what you long to do. And when he called out of the blue after our disagreement—fishing, I knew when asking how you've been—I chose to give him some of the good in your life rather than revealing anything about the turmoil you're struggling with right now. I simply shared how you were writing again because I'm excited for you. That's all. No plans, no pen names…"

My eyes welled with tears, and I grabbed hold of his scruffy jaw. "Everything about you is perfect, Aiden McNelis, and don't you dare allow the memories of that psychotic cunt of an ex-wife make you think differently."

"Cunt, huh?" He smirked, and I rolled my eyes.

"Can't you focus on something serious for longer than three seconds?"

"Not when your mouth is showing your naughty side," he murmured, lowering his face so his breath ghosted across my lips. "It's sexy as fuck, Padawan."

A shiver slid over me, and I couldn't even be bothered by the old nickname.

"Turn around."

"Why?" I asked even while he spun me and yanked me back against his chest.

"Because I want to give you something."

My hole clenched at the first thought that came to mind, but Aiden wrapped his hand around my throat, angling my face toward him. His other hand released my towel, and I jolted against him at the first stroke of his other hand over my dick.

I panted for breath, grabbing his wrist at my

neck. My eyelids fluttered shut. "Aiden," I whispered his name, soaking in the heat of him, the solid mass of muscle along my backside—his hard length digging into the base of my spine.

"One and only," he whispered back to me, his words hot against my ear. "I want all your firsts." Aiden stroked over my obscene erection, sending a shiver across my skin.

"They're yours," I blurted out, my hips thrusting toward his hand as goosebumps rose over my arms.

"I've had your mouth." He nipped my lobe, and I whimpered, pre-cum seeping from my slit to slicken his jacking.

"I've had this," he murmured, his grasp on my length tightening as his lips slid along my jawline toward my mouth.

"Yes...fuck, yes."

"I want you inside me, Jed," he whispered against the corner of my mouth.

His words...*fuck*, his words created an image in my mind I'd lusted over for years.

Cum shot out of me at the sight behind my closed eyes, and I squirmed, gasping.

"And I'm going to own you too," Aiden continued to spew wickedness, holding me upright while my dick pulsed my release. "Every hole."

"Yes." I shuddered, another shot of spunk milked from me by his firm grip.

"Every day."

Shit. I gasped and forced my eyes open, watching the final dribble of cum ooze from my slit as I melted against his hard chest.

Tension wound him tight, and I held onto his wrist with a death grip, panting.

He swiped the last bit of cum off my dick with his thumb and lifted sticky fingers. "Taste how sweet you are, then let me taste it on your tongue."

22

AIDEN

"**F**uck," Jed whispered, but he opened his mouth when I offered him my fingers.

I spewed curses as he cleaned my hand with his tongue, imagining him using his mouth on my aching dick.

Jed found his feet and turned, grabbing hold of my neck.

Leaning down, I captured his lips, tasting the saltiness of his cum.

Talking the talk was easy when it came to sex, and I got off at seeing how my words affected Jed, but insecurities over walking the walk still hounded me.

Kissing, no problem.

Sucking dick had also proven to be an easy feat considering Jed's inexperience.

And a hand job? Easy. I had just done what I enjoyed.

I wanted to promise him forever, to lay my life at his feet in exchange for the family he would lose—because he'd figured right. Choosing to fuck a man instead of worshiping God would cause an unrepairable fissure in the Simpson family.

Could I be his rock? Would I be enough?

Shannon's shit assured me I wouldn't be, but what if the problem had been hers? What if over the years we'd simply grown apart, began wanting and needing things the other couldn't provide?

My dick had become a bore to her, my kisses and affection tiresome—and I desired someone who would let me be *me* and allow me to love them in the way I'd always considered my strength. Handsy and snuggly.

She'd ended up hating both.

The thought of having what every human dreamed of, finding their person, infused hope into my shriveled-up heart. Potential for gaining such a relationship outweighed my fear enough that I considered trying.

Jed saw me as perfect, said he wanted it all, and even though I knew I was far from what he thought, his words and his willingness to take a chance encouraged me to do the same.

"Are you sure?" I had to ask before I lost myself in him because I didn't doubt once I got a taste of the wildcat who turned me inside out, I'd be done for. And if I fell short in his eyes and ended up even more jaded and full of hurt, having his firsts—being his one and only for even a short time—would be worth every agonizing second.

"I want you." Three simply whispered words set my mind on course, and I gave him my lips.

Offered him my heart.

I pulled Jed up into my arms, and his legs wrapped around my waist where they belonged.

My damn dick ached, stiffened to the point of pain, peeking out the top of my shorts. The weeping tip smeared across his perineum, and I shifted him closer, shoving my shorts down with one hand and kicking them off.

Thank fuck I hadn't stormed over in anything else.

Our mouths unlocked, and he stilled, our stares on the other's blown pupils. He held nothing back, allowing me to see him as he had on graduation night.

Lust overwhelmed his gaze, but tenderness lay beneath, emotion built upon years of close proximity and friendship. I didn't know Jed the man as well as I had the teenager, but I wanted to.

Inside and out.

Dick freed, I grabbed hold of his ass and spread his cheeks, gyrating my hips to run the back of my length along his crack.

His chest hitched up on a quick inhale, his nostrils flaring.

Slow thrusts teased the shit out of me, and I thanked God I wasn't lubed up and ready to roll, because I wouldn't have been able to keep from impaling him with every inch I had to offer.

I squeezed his ass cheeks around my dick instead, hissing at the dry friction—but I couldn't stop.

"Lube," Jed gasped, wiggling as though trying to do the exact same thing I wanted.

"No," I stated through clenched teeth, barely holding onto my sanity. "Not without prep time—I would split you in half."

"The fuck you would," Jed argued, tugging on my hair. "Sex toys, remember?"

The memory of his dildos…imagining him playing with his own ass… "Oh, fucking hell."

"I need your dick, Aiden." He shimmied from my hold and stood in front of me, slender, trembling… fucking beautiful. "You're going to breed my ass—fill me with your cum."

I shuddered, closed my eyes, and grabbed hold of my dick to squeeze the life out of it. "The shit you say."

He'd learned it from his wildcat and bear, but knowing he'd been thinking about me while getting off over their fucking…

Christ.

"On my bed." His bossy tone did funny things to my insides. I'd expected to lay him down and take my time loving him, but considering the porn he watched, I shouldn't have been surprised.

I sprawled on his Star Wars comforter, hands laced behind my head even though I was far from confident, my dick at attention and dribbling pre-cum onto my abs. Every cell in my body tensed, ready to explode.

He stared, running his gaze slowly over my entire body. "God, have I dreamed about this."

I bit back a grin when I caught him trying to discretely pinch himself.

A flick of his tongue over his lower lip, and Jed sprang into action, scrambling on top of me. His mouth went for my chest, his lips and teeth on my hard nipple.

"Ah, fuck!" I grabbed at his head, not sure if I wanted to yank his sharp bite away or hold him in place when he lathed at the sting that hit me like a punch of lust to the balls. Who the fuck knew pain could feel so fucking good?

"Goddamnit, Jed." I clenched my teeth and let him play, my hips restless in shifting, creating friction between my dick and his as he sucked the fuck out of my chest.

"So tasty," he murmured against my skin, running his tongue over the swell of my pecs, the marks he'd made, and back to the burning flesh he'd bitten. "I knew it."

Another bite, another curse from me, and the wildcat shifted lower, licking and nibbling every inch of my abs that contracted beneath his attention.

Suction from his hot mouth raised purple splotches across my stomach too—and I fucking loved the shit out of him marking me.

"Mmm," he murmured his appreciation of my taste, making my balls throb.

I lifted my hips to rub pre-cum against his chest, fucking dying for him to take me into his mouth.

"Jed," I groaned as his chin brushed over the leaking tip of my dick.

He lifted enough to get a good long look at my straining length. It jerked beneath his stare, and I fought off the need to tug his hair and force myself down his throat like he'd done to me.

A soft smile curved his lips, and he glanced up. Dark eyes piercing, full of want—and a little bit of wildcat devilry.

"No biting," I warned, my damn nipples still aching from his sharp teeth, the countless hickeys over my torso feeling much the same.

Holding my gaze, he leaned down and ran his tongue up my dick, lapping at the weeping slit.

"Fuck." Teeth clenched, I held tight to his hair, trembling to stay still.

"So good." He smacked his lips and went in for

another taste, but wet heat closed over the entire head rather than a simple lick.

"Christ!" My back bowed, eyelids slamming shut at his moan, the way he moved his tongue...

A first, he'd claimed—but Jed was a goddamn master at giving head. Even the slight scrape of his teeth couldn't ease me from the edge he placed me on after mere seconds of showing my dick the best loving it had ever experienced.

My balls fucking seized up, and I yanked him off me with a pop.

"Gotta...stop..." I gasped out the words, barely holding on behind my clenched eyelids.

More scrambling as he moved, but I lay tensed, grasping his comforter, fighting to keep from blowing a nut before he did.

The snap of a cap sounded, promising all sorts of wicked, delightful fantasies come to life.

Breathe...

His heady moan tingled the base of my spine. He stretched himself to take me inside his body.

Goddamnit.

Jed straddled my waist, his thighs bracketing my hips, and I forced my eyelids back open, needing to see him atop me. Drink in the sight of a gorgeous man who wanted me badly enough he set aside embarrassment to shove his own fingers up his ass.

Jed's dark sweat-sickened hair hung over his brow as he stared at me, his dark eyes hazed with lust. Flushed cheeks, parted lips reddened from sucking and kissing...

"So beautiful," I whispered, cradling his face in my hands.

He panted and let out a groan, his back arching as though he'd stuffed himself full with a third finger.

"Goddamn." I hissed and lifted my hips, the time for our slow burn to come to an end. "Jed. Need you—get the fuck on my dick. Please. Put me out of my misery. Can't fucking wait anymore."

He gripped my length with his lube-slicked hand, slowly jacking me, rubbing his palm over my sensitive head while I hissed at him.

"Jed..." I warned, teeth once more clenched.

A backward shift pressed my tip against his hole like the softest kiss, and he paused, giving me his eyes.

Zapping energy crackled between us, raising the hairs on my arms.

My ears rang. Breathe held as I drowned beneath the love pouring from his tender gaze.

"One and only," he whispered with a soft smile and slowly pressed against me, backing himself onto my dick.

His tight ring gave way, ripping all thoughts of rainbows and romance from my mind.

"Fuck!" I jolted, my hips snapping, slamming me

fully into his hot clasp. "Fuck—Jed, I'm sorry. Goddamnit, I'm so fucking...sorry. Shit!"

My head spun at the fucking perfection of being inside my Padawan.

So silky smooth..

Ball-throbbing, wet grip...

"More." Jed fucking *grinned* like a goddamn cat who found a bowl of cream.

"Didn't...hurt you. Fuck. Tight," I managed a few words from my blown brain that couldn't focus on anything but how luscious the inside of his body felt surrounding mine.

Still smirking, he ground against my groin, obviously loving the feeling of how I'd slammed into him if his blissed-out eyes didn't lie.

"You fill me so good, Aiden. Better than any dildo. Fuck." He moaned the curse, gyrating his hips forward and back, fucking himself on my granite-like dick.

It had been Shannon who tore my chest the fuck open with her poison, but Jed's words, his sensual movements over my body, stitched me back up.

"So, so good...I knew you would be," he murmured and leaned down. "Nothing feels better than this, Aiden. Absolutely nothing."

I lifted and took his mouth in a kiss meant for bruising. Desperate and hungry for him—the sweetness of his panted exhales, his spine-tingling moans, his slender form moving over mine like he was born to wreck me body and soul.

We rocked together as though of the same mind, my thrusts meeting his backward ones with increasing need until the sound of slapping skin mingled with our groans and curses.

Hot and tight, his hole welcomed my every jab like it couldn't get enough. The finesse of sultry dick riding became a lust-crazed cum chase.

"Nothing," I agreed and swore as he bit my lip. "Nothing..."

Jed speared his tongue back into my mouth, fucking mine like I did his ass.

I was going to come. Hard.

"Jed," I gasped and pushed him upright so I could grasp his hips to help him move. "Fuck."

I stared at his dick bobbing and leaking as I lifted him and jerked him back over my length. Wetness grew at his slit, dribbling—flicking as he arched and grasped my thighs, and I pummeled the hell out of his ass.

"Fill me with your cum," he groaned, a shudder rippling over him with every slap of his slender dick against his stomach.

"Fuck, Jed." I gritted my teeth, my hands surely bruising his hips as I held him still for my harsh thrusts. "Give me yours first."

"Oh, hell...yes!" He lifted on his knees and slammed down. Once, twice, in perfect time with me, and without a touch to his dick, cum spurted out of him, shooting all over my abs. "Aiden." He breathed a deep moan, and I slammed into him over and over, watching his beautiful cock release the pleasure he took from me.

So fucking hot...never knew... Fuck!

"Jed—" I came like a shooting geyser, my dick pulsing hot ejaculate deep into Jed's ass.

"I can feel you...shit, Aiden," he whimpered while grinding on me. "I can feel you—I want it. More."

My eyes rolled back into my head as tremors ripped through me, and I dug my heels into his bed, trying to go deeper. But it didn't seem to be enough. Jed kept moving over my length, milking me dry even when I shuddered and went boneless beneath him.

Too soon...I blew too fucking soon—

"Perfect," he murmured, cutting off my thought, his smile easing the rot in my head as he stilled and peered at me with sated eyes.

My fucking throat felt clogged.

"No." His grin widened, and he lowered himself onto hands placed beside my neck. "Better than perfect."

His eyes shone like a diamond in the blinding sunlight, glinting enough that an ache speared through my chest.

The best sort.

Happiness.

"Give me that filthy mouth," I said, grasping his neck and pulling him down.

Our tongues tangled in laziness as we caught our breath, his spunk and sweat smearing a mess between our bodies.

23

JED

A iden's kisses were life. His hands still gripping my hips the perfect grounding to my body that seemed to hover on a spiritual realm.

He'd taken me to a different plane, one where nothing but the senses indulged, where satisfaction and fulfillment left a man floating on a high better than any emotionalism from a pulpit.

Transcendent.

That was the word.

I smiled against his mouth, and he wrapped his arms around me, crushing me to his chest. "God, Jed. Why the hell didn't we do this years ago?"

Flutters lit in my belly as I buried my face in his soft neck. Citrus and musk filled my nose, my lungs, and a body-releasing sigh shuddered through me.

I'd always known we would be good together, but I never had guessed *how* perfect he would feel moving inside me. All the fantasies in the world, all the ass play I'd engaged in, the porn I'd watched while imagining him and me...not even close to the real thing.

His heart beat heavily against my chest as I lay wasted atop him. Eventually, his dick softened enough he slid from my ass, and I couldn't even move to keep his cum from dribbling from my hole onto his groin.

But he felt it, reached back, and ran his fingertip down and up my crack. "I want to see."

In a blink, I sprawled on the mattress, Aiden lifting my legs up near my ears.

"Fuck, that's hot." His lips parted as he touched my slick hole. "My cum looks right on you."

"It feels delicious inside me...leaking out of me."

He cast one of those single eye-brow-raised smirks that sent tingles racing over my skin. Holding my gaze, he glided two fingers right into my body through the mess he'd made.

Fuck, I was going to be sore the next day.

"Your ass is so hot. Loose from my dick." He hit my prostate, and I jerked beneath him.

"Shit—do that again."

My sexy Aiden gave me what I wanted.

Too sensitive...but fuck, his fingers felt good.

"Goddamn Energizer bunny," he said with a chuckle as blood slowly swelled me.

"Aiden..."

"Want me to suck your pretty dick?"

"I'd rather have you *sit* on my pretty dick," I told him, my face as hot as my skin from his continued stroking in my ass.

His pupils swelled, and he reached for the lube.

I swallowed hard, blinking. He'd teased me earlier about wanting me inside him, but I never would have thought he'd bottom for me. "What are you doing?" I asked, breathless, even as my dick twitched against my belly.

"Lubing you up so I *can* sit on your dick."

"Fuck," I cursed quietly—my turn to fist the comforter as he planked over me, his hand finding my hard length. "It's—it's not comfortable the first time something invades your ass, Aiden."

"Who says my hole hasn't been breached?"

Angry heat flushed through me at the thought of someone else touching him there, and he chuckled while continuing to make a slick mess of my dick. "Jealous of my fingers?"

"Shit." The heat remained, the prissiness over the thought of someone else having him first not fading even after hearing the truth. "Seriously?"

He slowly jacked me while continuing to smile down at me. "In the shower a few times over the years, but a lot the past couple of weeks while watching your two favorite porn stars."

Aiden positioned my dick upward, rubbing me up through his crack.

I let out a hiss and grabbed hold of his hips, all thoughts of jealousy long gone. No way I was strong enough to lift him like he did to me...

"Get on your back," I whispered.

He rolled without a single word.

And it was my turn to sit between his thighs and press his legs up. Lube glistened over his puckered hole, and my mouth watered. I smeared my fingertip through the slickness.

"Put your finger in me, Master Jed-i."

I shot my focus to his face, scowling.

"Jed, you're a goddamn master at playing my body."

Slowly, I breached into his heat with the tip of my finger. "No more Padawan?"

"Fuck no." He hissed as I pushed deeper, burying to the second knuckle inside his silken warmth. "Ah, fuck..."

"A single finger?" I pulled out and slid easily back in, twisting to rub over that sweet spot inside him.

"Jed! Fuck!" He jolted, and I repeated the action.

His dick lay limp, and I went to suck him into my mouth, but Aiden grabbed my face. "Leave it," he whispered, "and give me another one of your fingers."

I stayed bent forward, propped on one hand, working him open with my other. Our attention remained fixed on each other with an intense intimacy I'd never expected.

Even if my fingers hadn't been buried in his ass, we would have connected on a deep level. His passion-hazed eyes, recently sated, told me he felt the same.

I couldn't have looked away if I'd wanted to.

"I need you inside me, Jed."

Shivers licked over my skin at his haggard tone.

Always so shy, I'd never laid myself bare like I did while pulling my fingers from his clasp and pressing my dick against his slick skin.

Time paused as I held his gaze I'd always been scared of. Nothing but acceptance and need radiated back at me. No silliness, no weirdness, no judgment over my desire for him.

Aiden wanted me as much as I did him.

Breath stalled out, I slid into Aiden's body with one slow glide. I gasped at the tightness of him holding onto me, cradling me.

He hissed—and I bit back a sob, my heart threatening to burst with emotions I didn't know how to contain.

Aiden McNelis...mine.

All fucking mine—he opened himself up to me fully, crushing me to his hard body as I moved in him. Against him. Lips brushing with tenderness, his big hands on my ass, kneading, guiding me in how he needed me to love him.

Slow drags out to the tip of my aching length and a gentle rock back in, every rub against his prostate pulled rumbled moans from his chest.

"Christ, Jed...*definitely* should have done this years ago too. Fuck."

My entire body trembled from exhaustion, exhilaration, but my dick refused to rest. Hard and aching, my length filled him over and over in our sensual dance of perfection.

Too good...

"Aiden." I whimpered his name as my balls tightened, tingles racing down through my spine. I snapped my hips, hitting as deep as I could.

"That's it, baby," Aiden groaned. "Give me every inch of your pretty dick. Feels so fucking hot having you own me like this."

My eyes closed as I envisioned the sight of us—the same as that of my favorite wildcat and his bear.

But better.

A million times better.

"Swear to God, you send my soul soaring." Aiden's words swelled my heart with such longing to please him, to make him feel whole again.

His body clutched at me better than any lubed toy, the heat of his welcoming body, the way he sucked me back in when I pulled out...

"Aiden," I groaned his name, shaking, my eyes welling with tears.

"Can you come again?" Aiden asked, his fingertip dipping into my crack.

"D-don't know..." I whimpered, burying my face into his neck. My body moved on autopilot, fucking his tight ass even though I was ready to pass out from emotional exhaustion.

"I want your cum leaking out of me." Aiden's raspy voice pebbled my skin, his fingertip finding my still-slick hole. "And I want you to clean me up with your tongue then let me taste myself on your lips."

"Aiden." I groaned as he rimmed me, sending tingles through to the base of my spine.

"Yeah, baby?"

"Put your finger in me."

"Fuck." He gritted his teeth and ran his fingertip over my sopping hole.

"Do it."

He sank in without resistance, and two strokes over my prostate unlocked my release.

I arched and cried out, my dick jerking inside him. Nothing but gut-wrenching spurts escaped from my drained balls, but I saw the pearly gates of heaven. "Holy fuck, Aiden..." I gasped for breath, my body trembling as he slipped his fingers from my sore hole.

"Mmm." His chest rumbled against mine, and I went slack atop him with a shuddered sigh.

Hands roamed up and down my back, soothing every last bit of tension from my body.

"Can't move," I muttered against his sweat-dampened neck, beyond an endorphin high. Such peace and contentment filled me I could have breathed my last—a happy man.

"Then don't. Just stay right here." Aiden hugged me close, and I let out a heavy exhale and did as told, even after my soft dick slipped out of his body. Hard muscle and hot skin—I wanted to burrow inside Aiden and never come back up for air.

Eventually, our sweat and cum cooled, the mess more uncomfortable than sexy.

Aiden carried me into the shower where we washed one another, kissed, and hugged beneath the spray until I ran out of hot water. We toweled off and lay on my bed—the cum-stained comforter pulled back.

On our sides, we cuddled face to face.

"What are you thinking about?" Aiden asked, his fingertips trailing a lazy path over my back.

Since he'd finally gotten ahold of me, I wondered if he'd ever let me go.

He had needy—grabby—hands, and I loved both things about him.

"Honestly, I'm not thinking about much at all. Brain is too fried."

He grinned, his eyes more green than brown and twinkling.

"And you?" I asked, snuggling in closer to the heat of his body where I fit perfectly.

"Wishing I could go back all those years and give you more of my time. My heart."

"I wouldn't have bruised it."

"Like you did my entire torso?" Aiden chuckled, and my face heated.

"Not sorry."

"Good." He kissed my forehead. "I like your marks on my skin."

I ran my toes over his calf muscle, lifting an eyebrow.

"Fuck, your feet are cold!"

Chuckling, I pulled my toes away from his warm skin, thinking it was time for fluffy socks or a blanket since the heat of the shower had faded from my body.

"Sorry."

"Don't be. I like everything about you—even your cold-as-fuck feet." He yanked up the comforter and hugged me closer, and I pressed my nose to his bruised chest, breathing in the scent of his body wash. I hadn't held back in tasting every inch of his pecs, his shoulders—hell, his entire torso sported purple splotches from my mouth.

My dick miraculously stirred, but I pushed against it, simply wanting to bask in the afterglow, the satisfaction of finally being in his arms how I'd always dreamed.

"Put your feet on me, Jed. I'll warm them up."

Such a small thing, but I fell a little harder even

while he hissed as my toes made contact with his warm skin once more.

I nosed against his neck, my lips getting in on the slight action, trailing kisses over his scruffy jawline to the corner of his mouth.

We shared a gentle kiss, languid and gentle rather than hungry. Every stroke of his tongue was a memory I tucked away. Cradling his face, I pulled back, wanting to see the emotion in his eyes.

He stared up at me with such vulnerability, my heart ached. Emotion, the same I'd known I'd had for him for years swelled up inside me, a mirror of what I saw in his gaze.

"I—"

A knock sounded on my door, cutting off words that seemed too natural to say to him, verbalization of the connection we shared.

"Shit," I muttered, scrambling off my bed, adrenaline giving me a ton more energy than I thought possible.

Aiden sat up while I yanked on a pair of sweats, my gut going tight.

Another knock sounded, and I cursed again.

"Are you expecting someone?"

"It's probably my mom. She said she'd bring soup by."

"Fuck." Aiden started to get up, but I waved him back down. "Stay. Do *not* move from that spot until she's gone."

"Jed."

I turned in my bedroom doorway, hand on the knob, my pulse throbbing in my neck and making me light-headed. "It's okay. It'll be okay."

But I didn't believe the words whispered to ease the tension on my lover's face.

I held his stare until the door shut quietly between us. One slow inhale to help ease the panic in my guts, and I nodded.

I can do this.

I'd forgotten a shirt, but a third knock sounded, and I hurried through the kitchen area without one.

Help me.

Not sure who my mind whispered the prayer to, I pulled open my door.

"Mom." I couldn't find a smile through the raw nerves I felt sure flayed me open to her study.

She carried a container, her gaze flitting down over my half-dressed body. "How are you feeling, baby?"

I stepped back, allowing her entry because there was no way I could take the soup and send her off without a short visit.

"Um...okay, I guess." I wasn't about to tell her how my ass ached in the most delicious way possible.

She set the container on the table and turned, putting her hand on my forehead. "You're flushed and warm, but I don't think you're running a fever. Sit. Let me heat this up for you."

I gingerly sank onto a chair, knowing I had no choice while she puttered around, finding my pots without my having to tell her where they were. At least she had her back turned and didn't see my grimace as my ass met the seat.

Mom put the soup on and found my bowls and flatware. She settled across the table from me while I continued to struggle to breathe normally and pretend like I hadn't just lost my virginity—twice over, and that the only man I'd ever wanted still lay on my bed.

"I spoke with Renee after church this morning."

Of course she did.

I ran a hand back through my hair which was still damp from the shower, my heart rate kicking up even more.

"She's concerned for you, Jed."

Unable to meet Mom's gaze, I settled for studying the gray cotton of my sweats. "Why?" I asked because I couldn't avoid conversing.

"You've been withdrawn the past couple of weeks. Quieter without the kind smiles she tells me make her mornings brighter."

She'd often said the same to me. "I'm just tired, Mom. A little run down."

"Jacob told me and Dad that you're writing again."

I jerked my head up, annoyed he would talk about my private life with Mom, knowing how disappointed she would be.

"I'm glad," she went on before I could spout off in annoyance, and I blinked wide. "Writing your fantastical stories always gave you such joy."

"You don't think it will lead me away from my calling?" I asked, my tone still laced with aggravation even though she'd surprised the hell out of me with her admission.

"I don't believe mankind's sole purpose in the life God gifted them with is to live blindly by faith toward anything but Him. I believe He wants us to enjoy his creation, the time He allows us on this earth."

I sat and stared.

"Is it wrong for me to find happiness in my grandkids?" Mom asked, but she didn't wait for me to answer *of course not.* "Is it wrong for me to enjoy DIY shows instead of reading scripture while your father snores in his lounge chair every night? There's nothing wrong with loving things outside of God."

Her words reached deep inside me, and I wondered if I'd ever truly known my mom. "What about loving other people?" I asked, my tone guarded to my own ears.

Mom studied me for a few seconds in tense silence, and I held my breath, waiting for the questions I wasn't sure I was ready to answer truthfully.

She glanced over my bare chest—then at my closed bedroom door.

Fuck...fucking hell. My body tightened.

"It's not my place to judge." Mom gave me her full attention, and I couldn't look away even if I wanted to as her words filtered through my brain. "Every man will stand or fall before God on their own. My calling is to love others—and when it comes to my children," she stated quietly, leaning onto the table, "there's nothing you or Jacob could ever do that would make me love you any less."

Wetness welled in my eyes even as my heart continued its attempts to beat from my chest.

"I might not agree with your choices in life, but I would never—*ever*—turn my back on my babies."

A tear slid down my cheek, and Mom reached over the table to wipe it away. "You've loved Aiden since you were fourteen."

My breath caught as my heart stumbled.

"And only him since then."

I swallowed hard, wanting to nod but unable to.

"If he is who you love, if he is the one who completes you, I won't stand in the way. Neither will Dad."

"H-How can you know he won't?" I whispered, desperate for her words to be true.

"Because we watched you fawn over him as a teenager. Our hearts broke, same as yours, when he left for California, but we thought it was for the best when you chose the ministry."

"I did it for Gramps and Grandpa, not myself."

"Oh, Jed." Mom's eyes glazed over with unshed tears too. "We agonized over your reluctance to seek out love elsewhere."

"There is no elsewhere," I managed to say, "or anyone but him."

Mom clasped my hand, her smile wobbly, her eyes bright and watery. "Jacob won't understand. He won't accept it."

"I-I know." I sniffed, wiping more wetness from my cheeks.

"Is he worth it, Jed?" Mom asked, searching my face. "Is finally having your love returned going to be enough to see you through the sure dark times ahead?"

Words caught in my throat, and I glanced at my closed bedroom door.

24

AIDEN

I held my breath, my eyes clenched shut where I stood with my ear pressed to Jed's bedroom door.

Was I worth it? Was I enough?

Please, Jed.

I gritted my teeth against the tightness in my throat and the sting in my eyes as my insides shredded. He'd said there was no elsewhere, no other person, but...

Imagining his turmoil from being confronted by his mom turned me inside out, even though she'd been gentle, her words way more forgiving than I'd expected.

My heart ached for him even as my self-esteem curled in on itself, ready to die.

I clung to the memory of his bright smile, the satiated bliss in his dark eyes.

Fuck, just put me out of my misery already, Jed. I can't handle this shit.

"Yes," he finally answered. "He's more than worth it, Mom." Jed's voice broke on a sob, and I nearly burst through that damn door in nothing more than my skin and sink to my knees before him. Hug him. Bury my face against his belly and tell him I loved him.

Staying put twisted my guts into knots, but I set aside what I wanted. I wouldn't push, wouldn't be relentless in trying to make things right.

Jed had to do that on his own.

Things beyond the door went quiet for a few moments, and I strained, unable to hear a goddamn thing. Whispers—no voiced words. The scrape of a chair. The clink of flatware on a spoon.

"Mom—" Jed sputtered.

"It's okay, Jed," his mom said, her voice closer to where I stood.

Oh shit...fucking hell. I hopped back and grabbed my shorts off the floor from where I'd tossed them after our shower. Struggling to yank them up, I eyed the door—she had to know—there was no point in trying to hide in Jed's tiny closet.

The door handle turned as I straightened, facing the embarrassment of the ages.

No, no, no...

"Mom," Jed groaned, and a thump had me wondering if he banged his head on the table.

Shelly—Mrs. Simpson—filled Jed's bedroom doorway a second later, and I stood less than five feet away from her in nothing but my shorts. My pulse pounded in my ears as she glanced down over my body.

Fuck—the hickeys.

Heat rushed through me, my face without doubt redder than Jed's had ever been, but I remained firm in my stance, refusing to look away in shame. I loved the marks he'd left on me. Hell, I wanted to wear the damn things for the rest of my life—wouldn't even care if they landed above the collar line for the world to see.

"Well." She bit back choking laughter. "I see it's too late for me to say anything about practicing safe sex. You look thoroughly loved, Aiden McNelis."

Oh. My. Fucking. God.

"Mom!" Jed hollered from the kitchen, his voice a mortified whine.

"Ladle another bowl, Jed!" Shelly called out to her son, but no judgment shone on her face.

Her smile faded, however, and she stepped into the room fully, her soft palm cupping my scruffy cheek and making me feel eighteen again. "You've been like a third son to me, but I swear to God if you hurt my baby—"

"Never."

She pursed her lips, studying my eyes. "Be there for him."

"I will. Always."

"Good. He's going to need his person to hold him because it'll be some time before things right themselves—in the church and our family once they learn who his heart belongs to."

I nodded, knowing she spoke the truth.

———

"What the ever-loving hell *was* that?" Jed asked the second he shut his apartment door behind his mom. He blinked at me where I stood on the kitchen's far side, and I shook my head.

I wanted to laugh.

Curl up in a ball and hide.

Swing him around in my arms.

Kiss his mouth.

A slew of emotions rose up to the choking point in my throat as my heart soared.

His mom accepted me...would my own parents do the same? I expected they wouldn't give a shit since my sister had a girlfriend of her own.

"Oh my God." Jed buried his face in his hands, the tips of his ears a darker shade of red than his flushed cheeks a second earlier. "Kill me now."

"Hey." I strode to his side and wrapped him up in my arms, my elation and anxiety immediately calming. "One down." I kissed the top of his head. "And it went a thousand times better than I think either of us could have hoped for."

"That wasn't my mom," Jed muttered into his hands covering his face where he smooshed against my chest. "Honest to God, I swear an alien took over her body. What the *fuck*!"

Jed burst into laughter—until he cried and clung to me.

"Shh." I soothed his back as he broke down. "Come here." I lifted him up into my arms, and he settled in where he belonged, his legs around my waist, his wet face in my neck.

I shut off the stove, ignoring the simmering soup even though it smelled like home and comfort, and moved us to the couch where I sat, letting out a groan.

While Jed didn't have a big enough dick to demolish my ass, side effects of having something unusual shoved up there lingered. "I can still feel your dick inside me."

Jed snorted a laugh and slapped my arm but didn't pull away from how I cradled him on my lap.

Unlike my ex, Jed snuggled into me like a kitten, nosing me to the point I petted his nape, my happiness overflowing from my wide grin.

"I can't imagine your ass is any better," I said when I swore I heard him purr.

"Shut. Up."

Chuckling, I nuzzled his hair with my nose, loving his sigh and how he pressed in closer to my chest. "Are you okay?"

"I-I will be, yeah."

"Want to talk about it?"

"How long did you stay put on my bed?"

"For two seconds after you shut the door."

"So, you heard it all."

"Every word," I told him even though he hadn't asked a question.

Jed grumbled but didn't budge from my hold. "Nosey bastard."

"Yep. It drove Shannon nuts, and I can't imagine you'll be any different," I warned him, "but that's who I am."

"I'm glad you listened." Jed nosed over my clavicle as though sniffing me into his lungs. "I wouldn't be able to repeat everything she said anyway."

We were quiet for a little while, both of us chewing over our own thoughts. He'd chosen me fully, coming out to his mom, but how would he handle his dad? Jacob and Trish?

"Do you think she'll drop the bomb on the rest of your family?" I asked.

"She will tell Dad. There are no secrets between them, but she'll leave Jacob to me."

I wanted to push for answers of when I would be free to be with him publicly, how soon I could take him on dates, hold his hand, and kiss his lips in front of every person passing by.

"And Welker…"

I held still, my breaths shallow.

He exhaled heavily. "I-I need to confront him."

"Do you have evidence to base your suspicions on?" I asked, more hesitant than I'd usually be.

"Yes—the damning sort."

"Tell me."

I sat stunned and silent as Jed filled me in on everything he and Jamie had gathered. The hours they'd spent sneaking around offices, breaking into safes and locked desk drawers. Making copies at the local library rather than the church of everything they'd found.

One thick as hell manilla envelope of information was shoved beneath his mattress.

Jamie had a similar one at his home.

And a third had been sent to Ezra Jamison—an outside party.

"Do you want me to go with you?" I asked once Jed quieted, beyond spent and limp in my arms.

"And give Welker a reason to attempt blackmail?" Jed shook his head against my shoulder. "I'm going to do it the biblical way. I'll take Jamie as my witness. If Welker refuses to repent, I'll have to uncover his actions to the board and get their backing to do what needs doing."

"I say you just hand over that envelope to the board as an anonymous tip and allow the shit to hit the fan for that fucker."

"But what if Jamie and I are wrong?"

"What does the evidence say?"

"That we're right."

"Then why not protect yourself and let the chips fall where they crumble beneath his feet?"

Jed silently chewed over my suggestion for a few seconds, and I bit my tongue.

"Because," he finally stated quietly, "I submitted myself to him as a spiritual head, and I need to respect his office even if I can't give him that as a man."

"You're too good, Jed. He doesn't deserve to have you as his right hand."

"I have a feeling he won't much longer anyway. He's done wrong. I've done wrong—"

"We're not wrong," I muttered, knowing where he was going.

"Perhaps not in our eyes."

Our. I couldn't help my smile, and I hugged him closer.

"But others will see it as such. My choices lately are going to disappoint some people just as much as Welker's."

Pain laced Jed's words, dissolving the happiness I'd felt over his seeing us as something *right*.

I'd promised his mom to be there for him, and I vowed in my head to his silent God—if He heard— that I would be more faithful than any church member, any supposed Holy Spirit residing inside my man.

25

———

JED

I skipped going into the office on Monday and met with Jamie at his house that night. He appeared just as haggard as I felt. Worn down. Stomach rotted from anxiety.

He'd lost weight and all the color from his face.

Having used a mirror to shave the tiny bit of scruff off my chin and jaw earlier in the day after a make-out, jerk-off shower with Aiden, I knew I didn't look much better.

Jamie and I once more went over everything we'd compiled, and he agreed we needed to do what was fully right in the eyes of God.

Fully right in the eyes of God meant me giving up my male lover, the light of my life, the one I wanted to spend every hour with.

But I couldn't deny Aiden. Not in our lifetime, even if it meant an eternal one separated from God.

He was the oxygen in my starved lungs.

The coolness of sweet water on a dry tongue.

Sustenance to—

"Are you alright?"

I blinked Jamie into focus. "Yes." Clearing my throat, I began piling up the papers in front of me, fighting to put Aiden in the back of my mind. "Good. Yes."

"If I didn't know any better, I'd think I just caught you daydreaming about a woman, Pastor Jed."

I cringed—truly and literally cringed.

"Oh! I'm so sorry!" Jamie sputtered. "Forgive me, please. I just blurted the first thing that came to my mind. I've never seen you unsettled and flushed like that. Sorry." His words ended on a squeak as he sank into his chair.

I considered telling Jamie the truth, uncovering what he would understand as my sinful nature taking control, but I held my tongue. Strangely, not out of guilt. My insides twisted like brittle paper at knowing how he would be disappointed in me, horrified, even.

Jamie had always looked up to me as a spiritual guide, a godly man.

But I wasn't.

I was gay, I supposed I should label myself, and he would see me and Aiden as sexual perversion even though we were sexual *perfection*. The whole cliche about being two pieces of a puzzle couldn't be more accurate when it came to our minds, our hearts.

I tucked the envelope I'd brought along beneath my arm, and my attempted smile wobbled. "Tomorrow, then?"

He stood, lips tight, and nodded. "Tomorrow."

I got home—and went straight to Aiden's door rather than mine. He gathered me into his arms and for once didn't push for information, just stripped me down and snuggled me in his bed.

Warm hands, soothing along my spine. Hot breath and gentle kisses atop my head while I buried my face against his skin.

Delicious—but exhaustion pulled me under before my dick so much as twitched.

A hot mouth swallowing my dick woke me in the morning.

Best. Sunrise. Ever.

Aiden gobbled up every drop of cum I had in me, his sexy smirk and glinting eyes after I collapsed back on his mattress boneless making me smile too.

"You're too good at that," I said, expecting the truth of my statement would boost his ego.

He might act cocky as hell and tease me with every other word out of his mouth, but I knew what his heart needed.

And his body.

A memory of my wildcat and his bear flitted through my mind, and I held out my hand. "Come here," I said, and he obeyed, but I tugged him higher than my side, and he willingly straddled my chest.

"I might have a pretty dick," I whispered and flicked my tongue over the wetness of his slit, "but yours is sexy as hell."

He gazed down at me, his hazel eyes hooded with lust.

"Feed it to me."

"Your mouth..." Aiden shook his head and gave me what I wanted.

I gagged, choked, and sputtered, loving every second of pleasuring him, and when he came with a rush of cum down my throat, it was my name he cried out.

Head tipped back, tendons standing out on his neck, he came.

And came.

Master Jed, I was.

———

Jamie and I had made plans to meet in my office at nine-fifteen and head over to Welker's together.

But after telling Aiden about my evening with Jamie, how horrible the poor kid looked, I reconsidered. Knowing Welker as well as I did, I expected defensiveness. Arrogance. Denials and gaslighting. Toss in a bit of manipulation and narcissism, and Jamie would easily be crushed.

Wanting to protect him, I decided to do the deed on my own.

Tremors shook my insides like an earthquake, but I was as ready as I would ever be. He'd just arrived—I'd heard him greet Renee through my office door I'd left cracked open.

Steeling myself with words of self-edification, assurance things would go smoothly as long as I stuck to the truth of what the evidence showed, I strode across the reception area.

"Can you hold his calls for a bit, Renee?" I asked, my voice shaking.

A frown flitted over her brow, but she nodded. "Of course, Pastor Jed."

"Thank you." One last full inhale, and I rapped my knuckles on his closed door.

"Come in," he called.

I did as told, keeping my attention on the floor for as long as possible while attempting a confident stride across his office. I could feel his gaze land heavy on me, threatening to burst my heart from my chest.

"Good morning, Pastor Jed." His tone carried authority even with a simple greeting, and I fought to keep my breathing even.

"Pastor Welker." With trembling hands, I set the manilla envelope on his desk and all but collapsed into the chair across from him.

"What's this?" he asked.

I cleared my throat, hoping to keep myself from sounding like a squeaky, fearful kid. "I think it would be best if you look for yourself rather than having me explain." Damnit, my voice betrayed how my bowels churned.

I finally glanced up at Welker as he opened the envelope. The slightly dented brow of concern deepened as he pulled out the various papers Jamie and I had gathered. They held enough evidence to strip him of his title, his job.

A muscle ticked in his jaw, and red infused his cheekbones.

I doubted the color fed off embarrassment or shame with how much his scowl pulled down the corners of his lips.

Steady breaths did nothing to calm my racing heart. I clenched my fingers tight on my lap, my insides jittery.

"How many acts of invading privacy did you do while compiling this?" He shuffled through the papers with an unfazed air, his voice as level as when speaking to anyone seated across from him while I struggled to keep my shit together. "So many lines crossed...such deceit," he muttered and shook his head. "These records are kept inside a safe—the church's treasurer's to be exact."

Welker finally lifted his focus to my face, and I agonized over wanting to drop my gaze. "I'm sorely disappointed in your behavior, Pastor Jed."

As expected.

I lifted my chin, refusing to let him toss his shit back on me in whatever way he thought he could attempt. "I decided to be thorough in my investigation before approaching the liar behind this church's pulpit." Again with the damn shaking voice, but at least I got the words out.

"Liar?" One of his eyebrows rose, and he stood, angling toward one of the locked filing cabinets behind his desk I'd never been able to break into. "Let's talk about liars, shall we?"

He settled once more at his desk as though unhurried, a file in hand. "Jedediah Simpson," he read my name off the tab.

The blood drained from my face, but I lifted my chin high, knowing I had nothing to fear.

A bored flick of his wrist opened the file, and while a few scribbled sticky notes clung to the inside cover, it was the set of photos jammed inside it that had me leaning forward, my brow furrowing.

"You were quite cozy with Zeke Sipe while he worked here." Welker's tone held more than hinted suggestions about inappropriate behavior.

The image he peered at was one of me and Zeke in the church parking lot, standing close with our hands clasped in greeting. He and I had never been anything but friends. Whoever took the picture had captured an angle that could be seen as more if suggested in the way I knew Welker was capable of manipulating.

Heat rolled over me, tightening my stomach.

"He was my friend," I had no issue admitting to since our relationship had been purely platonic no matter what the photo could be taken as.

"Mmm," Welker hummed disappointment through his downturned lips as though he thought I lied. "And Levi Townson?"

"I hardly knew Levi."

"But you were together quite often—a bit...*intimate* for mere friends."

He tossed an image across his desk at me.

Yet another easily taken photograph on church grounds from a few years earlier during a Trunk or Treat event for the kids that his parents had helped coordinate. He and I stood with our heads together as though in deep discussion, shoulders brushing as he'd leaned into me.

"There is always loud music at those events," I stated, anger beginning to rouse through my nervousness.

"And this one?" he asked while pushing another beneath my nose.

Me and Ezra sitting in the church's cafe, taken when he'd still worked there earlier in the year. We too, sat close with our heads together—Ezra's hand on my forearm, my head lowered as though embarrassed or ashamed of his intense stare.

It had been the day before Welker had confronted him, and I'd been torn about keeping my mouth shut or giving the poor man a head's up about what awaited him.

Meeting Ezra's gaze for him to see and question my emotions hadn't been an option, and because of my weakness, it appeared we'd been sharing more than a simple lunch.

"And we can't forget Aaron."

Pictures of the two of us deep in conversation at the welcoming home party the church had for Ezra showed up next. I had my hand on Aaron's upper arm, and while it looked like I was feeling up all those muscles beneath his tight shirt, I'd only grabbed hold of him for a brief second to ask after Zeke and Levi as Ezra had ambled away.

But again, the angle suggested the former.

"All four men you've been close to over the years," Welker said, his tone lowered as though full of pity—and disgust. "All four perverted, gay sinners."

Faithful friends who show more grace and mercy than this church ever has.

The churning in my guts intensified but from the desire to take a lightsaber to his face, not fear.

I held his stare. "We're called to hate the sin but love the sinner—"

"Please, Jed. Don't attempt to preach to God's man."

I snapped my lips shut, knowing there was no point in arguing with his arrogant ass. The manilla envelope would have been better off delivered anonymously to the board, exactly as Aiden had suggested. I'd never been good with confrontation and arguments.

Why had I thought approaching Welker on my own had been necessary?

"I'm going to pretend I never saw this ridiculous attempt at a coup." Welker waved his hand with the same indifference his tone implied.

A coup? The man was mad.

"And you're going to go silently on your way." Welker gathered up the photographs that would be enough to make board members and church attendees question me if shown in the right manner—which their spiritual leader excelled at.

The burden I'd felt my entire life shifted—but became heavier rather than lighter. My jaw aching and head still at war, I stood and walked out on weak legs, leaving my evidence behind.

Welker didn't have to say, "Or else." I'd heard his threat clear as day.

I keep his secret, he keeps mine.

26

AIDEN

I got to the gym late and ended up working out alone since Michael had already left for the day. Preoccupied with thoughts of Jed and how he fared with Jamie and Welker kept me from doing much more than cardio and lighter weights.

My stomach remained tight long after I finished, and I waited for a text from Jed like he'd promised to send once he and Jamie finished their meeting with Welker.

Lunch came and went, and I couldn't eat a goddamn thing.

By two, I paced my apartment floor, my cell in hand, curses in my head while wanting to punch something.

"Enough." I stopped, swiped the screen to life, and shot off a text.

Me: **Everything okay?**

Ten more tense-as-fuck minutes passed while chewing the inside of my lip to absolute shit.

Wildcat: **No.**

"What do you mean no?" I growled, my fingers flying to text the same question.

Wildcat: **I'll be home in an hour. Fill you in then.**

"Fuck." I stared at his message, wishing like hell I could hear his tone, see his eyes so I would know what had happened.

Needing to lighten his load if he carried a heavy one, I went with the first silly thing to enter my head in the hopes it would at least make him smile.

Me: **Support you, I can. Comfort you, I will.**

I didn't get a response, which was telling as fuck.

My temples throbbed with every thump of my heart while I sat on the couch and agonized the minutes away.

Waiting.

Same as when I'd sent my ex that picture of her and one of her fuck buddies my friend had taken. I'd asked her what the fuck she was doing with her tongue down another man's throat.

She'd never texted back.

Just arrived home after her date she had told me was a business meeting and proceeded to inform me with attitude and disdain that she'd been fucking him because I'd never been anything but a boring, lousy lay.

Well, I sure as fuck knew how to please Jed—he made that clear as hell with every moan, whimper, and word leaving his mouth while I loved on his slender, beautiful body.

Fuck Shannon, and fuck Welker—

A knock jerked my focus to where it needed to be.

I hopped off the couch, telling myself Jed needed his own damn key while yanking open my door.

He slouched in the hallway, suit coat rumpled, hair on end as though he'd been running his hands through it.

But his eyes. Broken—

"Fuck, Jed." I lifted him into my arms, crushed him to my chest and, breathed in the hint of his shampoo that reminded me of the ocean and sunbathing. Sweet coconuts.

"Inside," he whispered, and I stepped backward, taking him with me.

A kick of my foot slammed the door shut behind us, and I settled onto the couch.

"Tell me," I demanded.

And he did. Every fucking word he could remember, fear in his eyes and tears coursing down his cheeks even as anger caused him to tremble in my arms.

I'd sensed his unrest for weeks, but to see him break beneath the strain weighing on his mind twisted my insides up.

And to know I'd only added to the stress with my teasing, my pursuit until he'd relented?

I felt like a steaming pile of shit fresh out of a dog's ass.

My chest ached. Eyes stung. Guts in a tangled mess, I agonized over being a part in his turmoil when all I wanted to do was make him happy, see him smile.

Long after he finished talking, I held him curled up on my lap. An assistant pastor still in suit, tie, and dress shoes rather than the fluffy socks he probably wanted.

My heart broke for him, and I realized he needed to set things right in his own head before we took another step forward. I refused to intensify his confusion, his anguish.

Even though the thought of stepping back, giving him space shredded my insides.

But if you love someone...

Fuck, this sucks.

I swallowed hard and forced myself to pull his face from my neck.

Wet eyes held mine searching for help, for assurance.

And I was going to break his heart—and mine.

"Jed." I knew what I needed to say but couldn't find the words.

Fear flooded his face, cramping my stomach. "Don't."

"I haven't said anything," I barely rasped, already hating that I needed to do the right thing for him.

"You don't have to." Jed scrambled off my lap, the loss of contact creating a gap just as deep inside me. "Are you done with me? Bored already?"

"No! Never!" I declared, horrified he would even think that. "But what we're doing in secret is tearing you apart inside. I can see it. I can hear it in your voice, Jed. Our being together is only adding to your anxiety, and it's *killing* me." I clasped at my chest, swearing the fucking heart beneath dried to a husk once more.

"I don't feel guilty about this," he said, his chin lifting even as it wobbled.

"I'm not saying it's guilt eating you up—it's the push and pull of everything you've built your life upon threatening to topple." I shook my head, my throat so damn tight I couldn't swallow, my eyes stinging. "I can act as your rock, Jed, but I can't be the reason you rebuild if you decide I'm what you want. *You* have to be. Your thoughts, your decisions. Not lust and obsession for the one holding your hand through this trial."

"It's more than just lust." Jed's eyes welled.

A tear slid down my cheek. At that moment, squashing my self-indulgence and putting Jed's mental and emotional health ahead of my desires made me realize how much he meant to me.

I loved him, wanted him above anything else in my life.

"It's the same for me too," I whispered my truth, "but you have to find your footing. I can't have another person dealing with regrets because they—" my voice broke on a sob "—chose me."

"I would never."

Shannon had happily vowed the same and had come to second guess herself.

I stared at Jed through my tears, desperate for him to understand my greatest fear, what I couldn't face happening again.

"So, we're...what?" Jed wrapped his arms around himself when I didn't respond. "Ending what we just found?"

My stomach heaved at the thought of breaking up for good. I ached to yank him back again me, to allow my Padawan to lose himself and forget what he faced. "This isn't the end but a pause." I gave what assurance I could, hoping like fuck he would figure things out sooner than later.

"For how long?"

My inhale shuddered through my body. "Until the war ends."

Hopefully, in my favor.

"But you're my escape..." Jed's voice trailed off, and my heart broke anew as the truth came to light in his anguished eyes. Tears rolled down his pale cheeks.

"Exactly," I whispered, knowing I had to force more words out. "And if in the end, you choose your God, if all I can be is your friend, then you'll have a faithful one for life."

We stared at one another in the silence, agony like I'd never known shredding through every cell of my body. More profound heartache than anything I'd experienced because of the deep connection he and I shared.

Tears dripped onto Jed's arms as he clutched at his torso, and I trembled with the desire to fold him up inside me, protect him. Win the goddamn war *for* him.

But I could gift him with something that would assure him of my loyalty—no matter the outcome of his decision. My legs weak from emotional exhaustion, I retrieved my extra apartment key from my kitchen's junk drawer.

"Here." I held it out, my hand shaking.

He stared at it a few seconds, long enough that anxiety spiked atop my heartache. "Why now?"

"Because you need assurance that I'll be here for you, Jed. Whenever and however." Another tear slid down my face as he took the key from my hand, careful to keep our fingers from brushing. "Always."

"I should go," he whispered, closing his palm and clutching it to his chest.

The anguish in his eyes when he lifted his head

ripped the oxygen from my lungs, and I bit back a sob that would break down my resolve.

I nodded when I wanted to beg him to stay. Did he see the truth in my eyes? Did he know that I would move mountains for him?

Jed tore his focus off me and turned away, my clenched teeth barely holding back the swelling tsunami of grief rising inside me.

The door closed quietly behind him, and I sank to my knees beneath the onslaught of pain, crying and cursing even though I knew I'd done the right thing.

27

JED

Pre-Aiden loneliness held nothing over how my heart ached with every dragging hour.

I could barely eat. Didn't sleep with the thoughts crashing in my head.

Jamie and I had met in my office after I'd confronted Welker as we had originally planned, and when I told him what I had done and that I hadn't mentioned his name, he'd sunken back in the chair with a heartfelt thanks, tension leaving him a heavy sigh.

I'd only shared with him that Welker had denied any wrongdoing, mentioning nothing about the possible threat he held over my head.

Keeping Jamie out of the battle had seemed appropriate, and I felt better for it. But that slight bit of goodness didn't stir a blip on the pulse monitor of my life as I went through the motions of work, hiding in my dark apartment, and crying while counting sheep at night.

Aiden hadn't lied.

I'd used him as my escape from reality, and the choice to avoid his door and not text him fifty times a day hurt worse than when he'd left for California. I thought I'd known love as a teenager, but those emotions paled in comparison to the ones eating at my insides.

He'd been an unholy temptation to my soul but had become the force behind every beat of my heart.

My eyes wept for the sight of him, my skin ached for his touch.

I was nothing more than a forgotten piece of a puzzle lost beneath a table and gathering dust.

No strength remained when Sunday morning dragged its ass into view, and I skipped church so I wouldn't vomit all over the stage while Welker took the pulpit in front of me.

Mom texted me within minutes after services started, asking if I would be over for our family dinner.

I wanted to say no, but the only way to figure my shit out was to get back to my old normal to see if it still fit. If *I* still fit—or if I even wanted to.

The house smelled like lasagna when I walked through my parent's front door, and my stomach actually growled. Both twins attacked my legs, twitching my lips upward.

A sense of home, of belonging swelled inside me.

"Son," Dad's smile while greeting me, his knowing gaze, held a moment longer than usual with zero trace of judgment. "It's good to see you."

My insides settled better than they'd been all week. Mom had told him about Aiden, and the truth of her promise over his non-reaction soothed me enough that my shoulders relaxed.

"Where were you this morning?"

Leave it up to Jacob's accusing tone to bring reality crashing back against me with sickening force when Dad's easy acceptance had filled me with peace I hadn't even allowed myself to hope for.

"Still not feeling well."

"Mmm-hmm." His tone suggested lips pressed tight, but I avoided his gaze while walking toward the kitchen with his kids wrapped around my legs.

They giggled with my every staggering step made in an attempt to move forward.

Talk about a metaphorical moment in time.

Trish hugged me, chiding her kids for bothering their sick Uncle Jed. "How are you?" she asked, holding me at arms' length after her kids scampered back into the living room. "Mom said you haven't been feeling well. When was your last check-up? Maybe you should have bloodwork done."

I hoped Jacob recognized the treasure he'd found in marrying her.

"Healthy as a bird, just without all the happy tweeting," I said.

She cupped my cheek like Mom often did while attempting to read my mind.

Of course, I shifted my focus off her to the tile beneath our feet.

"What do you need, sweetie?"

My man. My lover. My life.

"I'm just going through some personal stuff." I struggled to get the words out, wishing I could share the truth and be loved regardless.

She hugged me tight, and I blinked tears from my eyes as Mom looked at us from behind Trish.

Two oven mitts covered Mom's hands she held clasped to her heart. "Aiden?" she mouthed his name, and I shook my head, figuring she asked if he'd come along with me. Or maybe she wondered how we were. My non-verbal communication answered either way.

Trish released me, and a squeal from one of the twins and Jacob's resulting barking of an order to put something down pulled her from the kitchen.

Mom's turn to hug me, and I swallowed hard to keep from losing my shit right there in her arms. "Love you," she whispered, and I nodded, unable to voice the same. "Need to talk?"

I shook my head, stepping away from her hold.

"Maybe later." A shaky inhale, and I smiled. "Lunch smells amazing."

"You haven't been eating," she stated, glancing over my T-shirt and jeans while another ruckus sounded out of eyesight.

"Not much, no."

"I figured. That's why I made lasagna."

"You're the best." I kissed her cheek as crying started up in the living room.

"You can have Trish's jobs," Mom said, opening the oven door. "The bread and butter need to go to the dining room, then come back for the pitcher of ice water."

Five minutes later, my family sat down at the dinner table, both twins' eyes red-rimmed over whatever trouble they'd gotten into, but they sat quietly like little angels.

For the first time ever, we didn't share secretive winks.

Dad gave the blessing for which I didn't even close my eyes as my head bowed, and we dug in, the clinks of flatware on plates the only noise.

"Lovely service this morning," Mom broke the silence a few tense minutes into our meal, steering the conversation toward church and the sermon like usual.

The whole foundation of our family but definitely no longer the support and solidity beneath my feet.

"I've really been enjoying Pastor Welker going back to the basics of godly living this past month," Mom said.

Dad made his usual grunt of agreement.

"Today's, especially," Jacob said. I could feel his focus on me but ignored whatever he insinuated about my absence. "Making the right choices. Immersing ourselves in His word so we aren't easily led astray."

"And listening to your parents," Trish added quietly with a smile in her voice letting me know she spoke to her kids. Without a doubt, love radiated from her eyes while gazing at them.

"Pastor Welker is the embodiment of what it means to be a Christian."

I coughed over an inhaled piece of lasagna at Jacob's declaration.

Mom patted my back, and I drank down some water.

"He's the kind of man you look to for guidance, children." Jacob's firm tone made me cringe, his words stirring up disgust inside me.

If only he knew the liar behind the facade he encouraged his kids to idolize.

Wrong. So, so wrong.

I finally lifted my attention off my plate and glanced around the table, taking a long look at every face as they appreciated the food Mom had prepared, their murmurs hushing to nothing but buzz in my ears.

No wavering images of past Jedis hovered in the dining room, no echoing voices encouraged me to use the Force—but my chest expanded with energy, life-giving courage and strength as I took in the battlefield I faced.

My family wasn't my enemy, but they had allowed themselves to be led as sheep to the slaughter.

And not the type of sacrifice that set souls free.

Blinders shuttered their eyes to so much truth, so much love, that my empathy cup ran over.

I couldn't allow Welker to continue his deceit— with my family or the congregation who worshiped him like a god. While I didn't feel some of his flock who encouraged hatred for their fellow man were entitled to be set free of manipulation, they deserved the chance to choose their own truth.

"It's the work of demons, exactly as Pastor Welker said." Jacob's declaration snapped me back into the conversation.

"What is?" I asked, glancing between him and Mom as they shared a look.

"Homosexuality and lies are running rampant in the church, and it's all an attempt from the pits of hell to tear down what they see as a threat." Jacob shook his head and went back to his food. "Satan is trembling at the power of the Holy Spirit. In Pastor

Welker. In his faithful followers. In every single one of us who submits themselves to the pulpit."

Jacob's words echoed in my head, and I realized he spoke of those who hung onto Welker's robes rather than God's eternal ones where they should have put their trust and hope.

Unsettled didn't begin to describe the itchiness in my entire body.

I wiped my mouth and pushed back my chair, knowing it was time to go, to escape that particular battlefield since there would be no conquering by either side.

"Aiden?" Jacob asked before Mom could.

"If you'll excuse me—"

"You chose properly, Jed, but now you've lost your way and are fleeing the Spirit's probing to return to His flock."

Tilting my head, I studied Jacob's face, how his downturned lips revealed the same arrogance of the one he blindly followed.

"Things have shifted for me lately," I quietly stated, for once not feeling the need to look away from someone who wanted inside my head, "but as a believer, shouldn't you just trust God for my life? I had the same upbringing as you, Jacob. We share the same loving parents who taught us that very thing. But I still have the right to live how I see fit, and if pulling away to settle in my mind what I'm thinking and experiencing isn't acceptable in your eyes, then I suggest you turn your eyes the other way."

Jacob's face smoothed out, his gaze losing some of its hard glint. "I care about you, Jed, that's all. I want what's best for you, same as everyone else I love."

My throat tightened at the word he hadn't used toward me in longer than I could remember. However, lines needed to be drawn, boundaries I should have set into place years earlier to protect myself.

"If you truly love me like I love you," I said, searching his eyes and the hint of vulnerability he showed, "allow me my opinions, my life—same as I'll respect yours. We can agree to disagree for the sake of our family."

Mom sniffled, but everyone else sat silent, still as stone.

"My heart hurts to think you're choosing wrong and that you'll suffer for it." Jacob broke the hush over the dining room, his tone full of sorrow. He truly loved me, the poor misguided lamb.

"Then trust that God has a plan. Make that your focus if it will help keep a canyon from splitting us apart."

Our gazes held, and I clung to the hope that he would remember our childhood when we'd been inseparable, all the memories that bonded us.

"I'll try," Jacob finally said with a nod.

My heart felt broken and healed at the same time, and I struggled to force words out past the heavy exhale that eased the tension hitching my shoulders. "Thank you."

"Go on," Dad grunted from the head of the table. "Do whatever it is you have to do. Your family will always be here with open arms."

Tears slid down Mom's cheeks, but she smiled.

Trish's chin wobbled as she nodded in agreement with Dad even though she couldn't have a clue about what had gone down.

The twins sat wide-eyed and glanced around at the adults.

If I'd still been a praying man, I'd have lifted up a few for their impressionable souls. There was nothing for me to do but trust they both would somehow find the courage to make up their own minds about their parent's religion once they came of age.

At least Jacob hadn't gone with his dogmatism like I'd expected, and his choosing love over his God in that one area of his life gave me hope for his future.

My steps seemed lighter as I walked outside. The sun shone down on my head, rays of warmth and energy rather than what I had always considered God's fingertips offering affection.

The whole drive home, I considered the next

steps I needed to take and how best to approach the rest of my life.

While the battle raged around me, I'd found my focus, the strategy that wouldn't only free *me* from the shackles of oppression but dozens, if not hundreds, of others.

28

AIDEN

"What's bothering you?"

I'd been hard at the damn assault bike for a good twenty minutes of sprinting that left answering Aaron damn near impossible. Slowing my pumping legs, I gasped for air, my legs burning like a mother fucker.

Loving someone and letting them go hurt like hell.

"Jed shit," I muttered, still sucking wind. "Church shit."

"What's Welker up to now?"

I shot my head toward Aaron. He stood a few feet off to my left, arms folded, legs at a solid stance. "Not sure what all I can say, but don't be surprised if the church splits or he's at least—hopefully—kicked out on his manipulative, lying ass."

Aaron smirked. "I knew I liked you."

"It's been good making new friends—you, Ezra, Michael."

"Is that horny fuck still bothering you?"

"Nah." I grabbed a towel and mopped up my face before climbing off the bike. "He's a cool guy. It takes a lot of courage to do what he's done and stick to his new guns."

"Fucking massive guns," Aaron muttered.

"Speak of the devil." I nodded over Aaron's shoulder toward Michael who had just walked in the gym's door.

"I heard about what's going on at Simply Grace," Aaron stated quietly, drawing my focus back to his face. "Jed called Ezra a little while back."

"So, you understand the kind of battle he's facing."

"Yeah, and I don't envy the poor guy. Welker can be..."

"I only heard him preach once, and you don't have to speak another word."

"You like him," Aaron said. "Jed, I mean." His gaze probed, and I let him see the truth.

"More than like," I admitted. "He knows me better than anyone. Feels like my person if that makes sense."

"It does."

"But I let him go." I rubbed the towel over my sweaty head because I couldn't not move as pain ripped through my chest. "He's got his God, the ministry he's chosen. He also owns me and has the potential of a damn fine future."

"He can't have both."

I nodded. Aaron, I expected was well aware of what Jed faced in his head and heart. He'd gotten lucky with Ezra.

I could only hope for the same.

Michael exited the locker room and made his way toward us. "Where's that sexy preacher of yours, Aaron?" he called a little too loudly.

"Working at Humanity House. He's got set nine-to-five hours now."

"Talk to him about my threesome suggestion yet?" Michael joked with a wink. "Or the four of us." He motioned to include me.

"Not a chance," I said, snapping him with my towel even though he'd never follow through if someone actually agreed to an orgy. He'd given up sex because of how he'd associated it with his addiction for so long.

I had to give the guy credit. Not many men had the self-control to remain celibate when looking like he did—a bear of a man who was built like a goddamn immovable wall and had the face of a model.

"Still going to the meetings?" I asked as he hopped onto the bike beside the one I'd about killed myself on.

Michael's face turned a shade of pink I hadn't

seen before, and he immediately shifted his focus to the bike's screen to turn it on. "Yeah."

"Crushing on someone?" Aaron said with laughter in his voice.

I'd heard about Michael's crush on Aaron that had started years of bullying and how one simple act of contrition and forgiveness had set the two of them on a new path.

But I wondered if Aaron knew about Michael's celibacy. That question would have been a little cold in my opinion if he did.

Michael cleared his throat and started biking lightly. "There was this...hot twink at last night's meeting. He wears lip gloss."

"Get the fuck out."

Michael glanced over at Aaron as did I with the surprise in his voice. "He doesn't have a shy bone in his body, but he reminds me of you back in the day."

"Skinny as fuck, you mean," Aaron said, crossing his arms again.

"Yeah. But there's something about him...it's like he's burrowed under my skin like a goddamn tick after one hour sitting across from me, and I don't know how to dig him out."

The way Michael's forehead dented in thought, I wondered if he truly wanted the kid gone from his mind.

"Nothing wrong with making new friends—and you'll be ready to start over again someday," I tossed in my two cents, expecting Michael didn't have plans to keep his hands and dick to himself for the rest of his life.

"I suppose," he finally relented.

"Does this hot twink have a name?"

"Chase. He's moved down here from Boston for school."

"Wait," Aaron interjected. "Zeke's Chase?"

Michael shot a scowl our way. "Who the fuck is Zeke?"

Aaron burst out laughing. "Jealous much? Shit, man, take it easy."

"Zeke?" Michael pushed, not seeming to give two shits Aaron had called him out.

"My friend, the counselor—fell in love with Levi who was going to him for premarital counseling with his fiancée Lily. I told you their story."

"Oh, yeah." Michael's tone chilled out. "Could be the same Chase. I'd have to ask. Small fucking world if it's him though. I know he has plans to start volunteering over at Humanity House, and I was going to talk to Ezra to see if he could put in a good word."

"That's Zeke's Chase." Aaron huffed an exhale while shaking his head. "What are the chances?"

"He's a sweet kid," Michael said.

"Careful throwing that 'k' word around," I warned, thinking of how badly Jed hated when I used it. "Chase might not give you a chance if he finds it offensive and believes you only see him as a youngster who isn't anything more than a thorn in your side."

"Chase has the self-esteem of a goddamn gorilla," Michael said, "so no chance of that. How's Jed doing since I know you're talking from experience?"

I might have unloaded a bit onto my new friends. I also hoped Jed wouldn't mind if he ever found out I'd needed an outlet to help set my own head straight "Dealing with stuff at work, some family issues—I forced him to take a step back and decide what he wants."

Michael turned his focus off the bike's screen and studied my face, his legs slowing to a gentle rhythm. "You okay?"

"Fucking hurts," I said, shrugging. "I just want to be there for him, but this is shit he's got to deal with on his own. God forbid I influence his decisions and he winds up regretting choices and hating me."

"We're here if you need us." Aaron clasped my shoulder, and I nodded my thanks before he headed toward the front desk where someone waited for help.

"Did you already get a workout in? Sorry I was late this morning," Michael said.

"I killed myself on the bike but no weights."

"I'm going to warm up a bit more if you want to set up for back squats?"

"Sure thing."

"You made the right choice, Aiden," Michael

said, his legs starting to pump again. "Letting him go like that. If the two of you are meant to be together, it'll happen. Just hang in there. Don't go looking for an escape."

"No need to worry there, but thanks."

Michael nodded and set a faster pace, and I moved over to the racks, grabbing a barbell on the way.

I hadn't seen Jed since the night I'd sent him away, and while it had only been a couple of days, it seemed like an eternity had crawled past. It felt like a hole had been ripped in my chest—in my fucking life. Emptiness had taken over the place where Jed had made himself at home in my head and heart.

My sketching pencils and the magic he and I had created sat on my coffee table from the last time we'd worked together, our knees and shoulders brushing. I couldn't bear the thought of setting them aside.

It was his dream, and I would help it come to fruition one way or another—as his lover or friend.

There wasn't anything I wouldn't do for the man, and I hoped like hell he understood that.

I wanted to shoot him a text, had held my cell in my hand countless times to do so, even just to tell him I was thinking about him. My ears craved his voice, my mind needing to know how he fared on his battlefield.

Hell, I wanted to show him how much I thought

about him by sending a dick pic. The desire to poke and prod, find out the dirt on the church, his family, which way his mind leaned...it fucking consumed me.

I'd managed to practice restraint—but only because of him. Jed made me a better man, and fuck, how I wanted to gain the spoils and be the one holding his hand in the end.

29

JED

I walked into the church on Monday morning, ten files in my bag, a collapsible box in the other hand. My pulse thrummed, and the extra cup of coffee I'd sucked down due to a lack of sleep didn't help my jitters.

Nervousness had kept me on edge all night long, and dark bags hung beneath my eyes when I'd stared at myself in the bathroom's fogged mirror earlier that morning.

I could do this.

I am doing this.

Renee greeted me when I entered into the reception area, and I took the box into my office before returning to where she sat typing away on her computer.

"Board meeting is this morning."

She nodded. "Pastor Welker is running late as usual."

Good. I'd hoped and planned on that very thing.

"I'm going to head over without waiting for him, so if you could let him know?"

"Sure thing, Pastor Jed." She smiled up at me, taking a quick inventory of my haggard appearance.

I expected Mom would have an earful before lunch.

"Talk soon," I muttered and hurried out of the office before she could ask if I was okay.

Heart pounding, I strode down the hallway toward the main conference room the board met in once a month. Having agonized over how to proceed the night before, I didn't have to wonder anymore.

I'd asked myself who the most self-righteous, legalistic man on the board was and came up with that answer immediately.

Mr. Townson, Levi's dad.

He would stick to the letter of the law, and he wasn't a man easily swayed.

While an asshole toward his son, one who didn't show grace and mercy as the Bible commanded, he would feel peaceful—hell, probably find joy—in pointing out the splinter in Welker's eye.

Even if his plank was big as fuck as far as I was concerned.

I had all of five minutes before Welker arrived if he kept to walking in after the church's board members were seated and waiting for him like he was their king.

And I would make the most of it.

Everyone sat at the table—on time as I'd known they would be, and heart in my throat and hands shaking, I nodded at their greetings and pulled out the files.

Each of the eight men didn't speak a word as I silently handed them out. As if they'd felt a shift in the room from the anxiety I'd brought along with me, quietness of tongues and spirit descended.

I laid a folder in front of Mr. Townson last, choosing to remain on my feet beside him rather than sit in my empty chair on his left.

He studied me as the shifting of papers began around us. Two gasps—one man took the Lord's name in vain.

Mr. Bowers, the treasurer, I had no doubt, but I didn't give him my attention.

I swallowed hard while holding Mr. Townson's gaze. "With your faithfulness to God and loyalty to the law strong enough you turned your back on your only son," I said, my voice shaky as hell over finally having a chance to get a good dig in at the asshole, "I know I can trust you to do what's right with this as well."

Mr. Townson cast his focus off me at the mention of Levi, and if I didn't know the man any better, I'd have thought he felt a bit of remorse for his actions.

Perhaps there was hope for him and Levi making amends one day—but I wouldn't hold my breath.

He flipped open his file, but I continued.

"But just in case you all decide to sweep this under the rug, plenty more copies of this evidence exist, and I'm not above ensuring this information is released to the thousands of people who have supported this church and its leaders for dozens of years."

Hands shuffled through the papers, rubbed at jawlines, but not a single man lifted their focus toward where I stood looking over them.

Mr. Bowers sat back in his chair, face pale, hands on his lap.

There was no way he could say a word of denial that wouldn't be an obvious lie. He also didn't have the manipulative sway or anger that Pastor Welker did.

"I'm offering—"

The door opened cutting me off, and Pastor Welker walked in, a grin on his face. At the heads lifting, the stares he received, all color fled his cheeks.

His gaze shot to me where I stood at the opposite end of the room. "Pastor Jed." Actual fear laced his tone, and I wanted to jump up and down, my hands raised in victory.

"Pastor Welker." I nodded a greeting. Red rose to mottle his face, but I cut him off before he could start spewing bullshit. "To those of you on the board"—I turned toward the men whose faces ranged from white to near purple, their gaze flitting between me and the man they'd chosen to blindly follow—"I'm offering my official resignation."

"Pastor Jed—"

I held up a hand, stopping Mr. Townson regardless of his murmur of my name. "You have what you need to do what's right in the eyes of God—and man. My assistance is no longer required, and I have no wish to prolong the inevitable."

I approached Welker who stood in my way, and his glare would have normally made me cower or turn my face away at the very least. Lifting my chin, I moved into his personal space, and when he didn't step aside, I smiled, my insides twitching.

"You'll pay for this," he seethed quietly, his coffee breath wafting over my face.

"Unlike you,"—I gave him my best disdainful once-over and bored expression—"I haven't broken any of man's laws and have nothing to fear."

"But you've broken God's." His dark eyes glinted with hatred as he leaned down closer to me, his voice nothing more than a hiss. "And you'll spend an eternity burning in hell."

"Then I expect I'll see you there." I had the balls to slap his shoulder like we were old pals before scooting around him.

"Gentlemen," I called over my shoulder while

standing on the threshold, "I hope the true meaning of Christianity and following God's commandments will guide you in moving forward."

I walked out. Closed the door with a soft snick—and released the shakiest exhale known to man.

I did it— I fucking did it.

That damn burden hanging on my shoulders was gone. Dissipated into nothing.

My war had been won with a simple choice.

And I'd thought my feet left the ground when Aiden had loved on me our first time together. Elation wasn't the word for the lightness in my chest, but I couldn't come up with another for the sense of freedom I felt rushing through my body.

Grinning, I hurried back toward the office area, hoping like hell the board kept Welker occupied while I packed up my shit and got the hell out of Simply Grace.

Renee took one look at my face and stood, hand flying to her chest. "Jed, what's wrong?" She glanced behind me, but not seeing anyone on my heels, she turned toward me.

"Plenty of gossip will hit your ears soon enough," I told her, striding toward my office with my grin stuck in place. After the depression, she'd watched on my face the previous few years—heightened the past couple of weeks—I expected she thought I'd gone manic.

She followed on my heels, but I didn't offer any further information. "You're...leaving?"

My tossing stuff into the box couldn't be taken any other way. "I am."

"They know the truth," she whispered, and I paused from emptying my desk's top drawer, giving her my full attention.

What Welker had been doing? About me? If Renee knew, the entire staff would have found out.

"The truth about...?" I asked, drawing the word out, unbothered by however she might answer where a couple of days earlier, I'd have been riddled with fear.

Renee glanced at my open office door behind her. "That you're gay and have loved Aiden since you were fourteen," she whispered behind her hand.

So, my situation—not Welker and the treasurer's thievery.

I tossed something into the box and straightened, my hands on my hips. "Why don't you tell me who *they* are since you're so sure you have inside knowledge?"

She bristled at my insinuation, but I didn't care if she was Mom's best friend.

"I've known since you were little, Jedediah Simpson," she hissed but sounded more like wanting to keep quiet rather than angry at my suggestion she was a gossip. "I do enjoy chatting a bit too much, but I would never uncover your sins—"

"It's not a sin to love another man," I cut her off, returning to my job so I could get the hell out of there. "What I feel for Aiden isn't sexual perversion. It's too beautiful, too peaceful—too right in my heart and soul to be wrong."

She didn't reply, and I glanced up to find her eyes welled with tears.

"How long have you known?" I asked.

"Since that first Sunday Aiden came to church with your family all those years ago."

"I was that obvious?"

"You looked at him like he'd brought vibrant color to your black and white life." Her words sounded like poetry—the kind I'd been blessed to live.

Aiden had always been the brightness in my existence, even after he'd left for California, the memories of him had kept a flicker of spirit inside my chest.

Only him.

My…rainbow of sorts.

Smirking, I picked up the few personal belongings on the top of my desk and piled them on top of the things already in the box.

"Where will you go?" Renee asked. "What will you do?"

"Start over," I didn't hesitate to answer. "And as long as I have Aiden by my side, I don't care how the rest pans out."

Renee wiped at her eyes, crossed my small office, and pulled me against her soft bosom, same as she'd done quite a few times when I'd been a kid and had needed comfort when Mom hadn't been around.

"I hope you're happy, Jed. Always."

"I will be." I knew that truth in my heart. Even if things didn't work out with Aiden, I'd finally chosen to be *me*.

And I couldn't wait to begin.

30

AIDEN

I stood in the shower, resting my forehead on the cool tile, scalding water beating on my sore muscles. Michael and I had pushed ourselves at the gym, and having started with that damn bike, I didn't have much energy left.

Jell-O legs, a shaky mind, unsettled emotions...I was a fucking mess. All I could think about was Jed—how he fared at work, where his current head-space had taken him.

I shut off the water and dried my body, scowling at my scruffy reflection. Telling myself I hadn't made a mistake by pushing him away didn't lessen the unease inside me.

That whole if you love them let them go shit... what if your love wanted you, your strength, your support, and you stepped back at the exact moment they needed you most?

What if I'd made the wrong fucking decision by forcing Jed to face the music alone? What if having my shoulder to lean on would encourage him to speak up? What if my hand clasped around his was what would give him the confidence to face down his family and stand up for himself?

"Fuck." I scrubbed a hand over my clenched jaw.

Or did I only second guess myself because of how I ached for him?

I hurried out of the bathroom, intent on my cell I'd left atop my bureau to find out for sure. A knock sounded, and I detoured—but the sound of a key sliding into the lock made my heart race and pulled me up short of the kitchen.

Only one person had a key to my apartment.

He opened the door, gaze snagging on the towel wrapped around my waist.

"Jed?" A good twelve feet separated us, but I could feel his gaze like a caress, his presence like a summer breeze.

The door clicked shut on its own behind him shutting us away. Together. Alone.

Pink fused his cheeks to the tips of his ears, but it was the clearness in his eyes once they returned to my face that stole my breath and set my pulse to thumping.

He dropped his bag—straight from work, I realized.

He shed his suit coat and kicked off his dress shoes, holding my eyes the entire time.

Yes...fuck, yes.

I couldn't fucking breathe.

My dick tented the towel as he ripped his tie off.

That look in his eyes...I'd seen it once before, and I braced for the impact even while adrenaline rushed through me, making everything brighter. Clearer. More vivid to all my senses.

He came at me like a whirlwind, climbing up my body. "Choose you." His mouth slammed onto mine, but I didn't need any more words.

My heart soared, and I crushed him to me, holding on for dear life. Jed horny and uninhibited was a fucking gorgeous thing. Hungry lips, panted breaths with whimpers that seeped pre-cum from my dick. Grasping hands pulling at my hair, fingers digging into my back and shoulders.

And his tongue—fuck, his luscious tongue sliding over mine, tasting and fucking.

I needed inside his ass.

Yesterday.

"Jed," I groaned as he nipped my lower lip, allowing me to snag a lungful of oxygen.

"Went to the board," he said, scrambling down as fast as he'd climbed me. Buttons pinged from his dress shirt as he struggled to tear it off with shaking hands.

I helped with his belt, yanking it from the loops

before damn near ripping the material to get at his dick.

"Oh, God." He groaned when I clasped him in my hand, kicking his socked feet to rid his legs of his dress pants.

"You went to the board," I reminded him where he'd been going a few seconds earlier, my hand smearing pre-cum down his length.

"Yes, with the evidence." He gasped as I squeezed.

"Welker outed you after?"

"I'm sure he did." Jed panted, his hands on my shoulders, head tipped back to hold my gaze. Black ate at the brown of his eyes. "But I shut the door in his face before he could so I wouldn't have to hear it."

"My brave little Padawan."

"Your *ballsy man*," Jed corrected me and let out another groan as I fondled his soft sack.

"Mmm," I hummed my agreement, rubbing my nose over his. "I do like your balls."

"I don't care—about Welker outing me," Jed hastened to correct himself, tipping his head so he could see my eyes again. "For the first time in my life, I feel free. There's no burden on my shoulders, and nothing is going to hold me back from living. From loving." He swallowed hard and licked his lower lip. "If you'll have me."

"If I'll have you." I snorted, stroked him one last

time, and slapped his bare behind with a pre-cum sticky hand. "Get your cute ass in my bed where you belong."

"For how long?" he whispered, his feet not moving like I'd have preferred.

"A solid seven and a half inches." I winked, and he scowled up at me. "For however long you'll have me," I told him the truth in my heart.

His face relaxed, happiness shining in his eyes. "That'd be for eternity," he said, stealing my breath and leaving me speechless.

I stared after him as he hurried to do as told. His ass flexed with every quick step—those goddamn dress socks still clutching at his feet.

Probably *cold* feet.

My Padawan needed me.

I stalked after him into my bedroom but detoured for my bureau and the top drawer as he hopped onto my bed. I grabbed what I wanted and turned to find him sprawled out like an offering, lube beside him ready and waiting.

A feast.

"All mine," I murmured.

He shivered, goosebumps rising over his skin as I took my time checking him out from heaving chest to those damn socks. I moved closer, hitching his breath—and peeled the thin material off his right foot.

"Cold," I murmured, kissing every toe, sliding my

tongue between them. Nibbling and sucking until he grew restless. "Ticklish?"

"No."

"I love these cold toes." One last kiss and I slid a fluffy sock over his foot.

"My favorite Boba Fett fluffies! Where'd you get those?" he asked.

"Mmm." I gave his left foot all my attention, hoping he'd forget his question.

"Were you snooping in my bedroom again?"

I chuckled, no longer feeling like a creep over what I'd done weeks earlier. Had I kept to myself rather than poking into his private life, I doubted we'd have gotten as far as we had in so short a time.

It'd been the sight of his toys that made the wheels turn, and the bear and his wildcat that had taken us past the point of no return.

"Yes, I poked around and stole them—and I might have jerked off with their softness wrapped around my dick."

"Why is that hot?" Jed groaned while I covered his left foot and set it back on the mattress.

I finally dropped my towel.

His focus dipped down to my straining dick as I slickened my flesh with lube. "Forget the socks and forget seven inches. You're a solid nine, at least."

I barked a laugh and crawled between his spread legs, staying on my hands and knees atop him. "Not quite, but I'll pretend for your sake."

One of my lubed fingers found his sweet hole.

"You're perfect, Aiden McNelis," he said with a whimper while I slid a fingertip into his hot body.

Lowering my head, I nosed along his smooth jawline to nibble on the corner of his lips, all fear of disappointing him as far from my mind as my divorce was in the past. "Only for you."

I pushed in deeper, readying him to take my dick, and he whispered a drawn out, "Fuuuck," that dripped pre-cum from my slit. "More...please, Aiden."

"So hot." I scissored and reached deep into his silken heat. "Never expected to feel you here...feel you in my soul."

Jed wrapped his arms around my neck and ankles around my thighs, pulling my weight down atop him. "Since the age of fourteen, I've known you were it for me. I just never thought I'd have the chance to experience the life I've always longed for."

Emotion poured from his eyes, the kind that lit fires and blazed forests to ash. But I could trust Jed with my heart. He would never leave me in ruins. He was a gift I didn't deserve, a second chance I never expected fate would offer me.

Warmth swept over my skin, the energy rippling between us with undeniable, life-bestowing force.

"Love me, you do," I couldn't help but tease, giving him the twinkled-eye look that always made his face red.

The happiness in his eyes, the flush on his face, filled my heart to overflowing. "Yes," he whispered and lifted his head to kiss me.

No shrill voice echoed in my mind as I planked and slowly pushed my dick into Jed's body.

"Christ, are you tight." I clenched my teeth, eyes rolled back into my head.

His thighs clasped at me, fluffy-covered feet latching around my legs, holding our groins tightly together. My balls throbbed, my dick twitching deep inside his ass.

"Want all of you," he whispered up at me while I shook from the need to fuck like an animal when I'd planned to make love.

"You have it—every inch." I went with teasing to keep from blowing too soon.

"Bastard," he muttered with a grin.

"And you love it."

"Hell yes, I do. Come back down here."

I gave my bossy little wildcat what he demanded, lowering most of my weight atop him.

His moans filled my ears, and his mouth bruised my neck and shoulders as I rocked in and out of his tight ass. We fit together so goddamn perfectly I almost cried.

Nothing felt better than loving on Jed. His words of edification, his grasping hands...the whimpers then sobs when I finally took his leaking dick in hand.

"Yes...*please*, Aiden."

I stroked him in time with my steady thrusts, watching him come undone beneath me. Shivering and shaking.

Breath held, his eyes latched onto mine, and he bowed his back. "Aiden," he cried out my name, and spunk shot up over his chest.

"Love you, Padawan." I gasped out, my hips moving on their own, chasing release inside his contracting ass. "So. Fucking. Much."

He grabbed my face and pulled me down, our mouths coming together as my balls released. Heat flooded through me, tingling my skin, my spine.

And I kissed Jed with every bit of affection and appreciation I had swelled up inside my heart he had healed.

31

JED

ONE YEAR LATER

A short aisle lay beneath beams of the sun rather than a long one down a church's center, and a string quartet played quietly instead of an organ's shriek.

My entire family sat on folding chairs waiting for the "bride"—Jacob included—while I fought for calm in front of them. He still didn't believe the love Aiden and I shared was godly, but he'd never once condemned or ranted against homosexuality in front of us.

Simply Grace Church had split as expected in the months following Welker's arrest, and a new, younger pastor took over the buildings and those who remained faithful to God—my parents and brother included.

The day school lost some of its students, but Jacob retained his job, thank goodness.

He'd also climbed on board the 'Uncle Jed is a published author' thing his kids squealed about. Within a matter of months of working hours on end, Aiden and I had completed two graphic novels.

And both hit YA bestseller lists on every retailer, pre-orders for books three and four cresting triple digits.

While we hadn't raked in the cash, the call we'd gotten the week from a Hollywood exec interested in movie rights suggested that might change.

I didn't care if we never became household names for kids' sci-fi graphic novels, but if our shared passion at least provided us enough to live together without too many monetary worries, I would be a content man.

Mom had been our biggest supporter, making a list of all the booksellers in the Philly area and going to every one to coerce them into carrying her sons' books.

She cried along with Trish while watching me wait for my man, and even Dad swiped the back of his hand over his wet eyes.

Aiden's parents, his two sisters, and a handful of friends sat opposite my family. Zeke and Levi had driven down from Boston, and Aaron and Michael along with a few other gym rats attended as witnesses as well.

I'd never been so accepted, so loved. I imagined it was what the Force truly felt like—a flood of energy, zapping cells with life, an overwhelming need to flow and visually make itself known.

I supposed everyone would have expected me to walk down the aisle to Aiden, but I'd fantasized about him in a white tux, pinning me with his hazel eyes while I waited dry-mouthed beside whoever would bind us together for life.

My dream sort of came to fruition that summer afternoon.

Aiden appeared in the distance, stealing my breath and making my already weak knees want to buckle.

He wore black instead of the color of purity while striding toward me with hooded eyes, and I'd never seen such a hot sight. He'd sucked me down earlier that morning in the hopes of keeping me from popping a boner, but damn, my man looked like a feast.

He peered at me like he thought the same about me in my own black tux.

I salivated rather than craving water, his every step closer making my heart race.

Ezra stood behind me to bind me and Aiden together in unholy matrimony, and once my lover reached my side, I lost track of people, time, and space as our hands came together.

Solid. Warmth.

My strength.

Hazel eyes, more green than brown studied my

face, a hint of a smirk in them also tilting his lips I couldn't wait to kiss.

Ezra spoke about love and commitment, but I lost myself in Aiden, not having an ounce of desire to look away from him. He'd captured me heart and soul, and I could easily spend the rest of my days gazing into those eyes that enticed butterflies to fly in my stomach.

We spoke the vows we'd written to one another, mine a bit more flowery while promising to love him in sickness and in health.

And he joked about submitting to his Master Jed-i which roused our guests to snickers and laughter.

He enjoyed my bossy ass, but no true dominance or submission entered into our relationship. We both gave and took, equally unselfish in our desires to fulfill the other.

Even outside our bed, Aiden offered affection, subtle touches while we worked side by side and his fingers threaded to mine while we snuggled and watched movies together.

I'd been starved for so long, and he was the well that never ran dry.

My love, my life.

"I now pronounce you husband and husband." Ezra's low voice pulled me from where I'd gotten lost in Aiden's eyes.

My heart exploded as Aiden brushed his lips over mine.

A few shrill whistles broke out along with applause.

Such peace rolled over me that my eyes welled.

"Okay?" Aiden asked quietly, his gentle smile and shining eyes etched into my memory forever.

"Incandescently happy."

Chuckling, he tucked my hand in his arm, and we escaped back down the aisle, a blur of smiling faces registering through the haze covering my eyes.

But the sweetest part of marrying my best friend? It was our first dance to Malachi and Isaac's newest chart topper.

Forever Mine.

"All those times making love to you," Aiden bent and whispered close to my mouth while we swayed with the duo's perfect harmony spilling from the DJ's speakers, "I never thought anything could feel better. But this?" He took my left hand and kissed the ring he'd placed on my finger. "Knowing you're really mine, heart, body, and soul?"

He filled his lungs and let out a contented sigh before kissing me softly.

"You're the best man for me," I told him, clutching at his sides and having to arch my back to see his face with how close we danced. "You're the other half of the puzzle piece of my life."

Those twinkling eyes welled with unshed tears. "Christ, do I love you, Padawan."

I pinched him lightly, even though I'd actually come to like his pet name.

"Your weirdness, your love of fluffies and Star Wars," he continued. "Your cute little toes that taste so damn delicious."

Laughter bubbled up inside me.

"Even your cold feet seeking the warmth of my body when we're in our bed."

He didn't lie. My Aiden never jerked away when I found myself chilled. His grabby hands pulled me close, holding whatever part of my body that needed him most.

"You're perfect, Aiden McNelis," I reminded him of what I often did because he could never hear it enough. "All nine inches of you."

Aiden chuckled, his hands lowering toward my ass.

"Behave."

"Never, wildcat," he whispered hotly against my ear, sending a ripple of goosebumps over my skin.

"I love you for more than just your dick and this chest I'm going to cover with hickeys tonight." I ran my hands over his pecs, anxious to rip the damn tux off him to get to all the delicious skin hiding beneath. "This is what's most precious to me." I laid my hand over his heart, knowing mine shone in my eyes. "How accepting you are. Loyal. Protective..."

He kissed me as though my lungs held the breath he needed to survive.

"My husband," I breathed over his mouth the second he allowed, a sigh shuddering through me. "My one and only."

THE END

———

ABOUT THE AUTHOR

Lynn Burke is an international bestselling and award-winning author. A stay-at-home mom, she's a lover of coffee and vino, and with three spawn and two fur babies underfoot, noise levels dictate the daily switch-over time. In her few quiet 'me' moments, she can be found hunched over her Mac, trying to type as fast as her muse spews hot stories.

You can find more about Lynn at her website: www. authorlynnburke.com

ALSO BY LYNN BURKE

Abel's Obsession

Divulging Secrets

Healing Storms

In Between

Reluctant Lumberjack

Resisting his Mate

The Playboy Bachelor

Billion Dollar Love Anthology

Blood Born Series

Bonds of Worship Series

Dark Leopards MC

Darkest Desires Series

Devil's Outlaws MC

Elite Escort Series

Fallen Gliders MC

Forbidden Obsession Duet

Found by Fate Series

Midnight Sun Series

Missing Link Series

Risso Family Series

Sandy Ridge Series

Sinful Nature Series

Vicious Vipers MC